THE CASE OF THE
DIAMOND
DOG
COLLAR

THE CASE OF THE
DIAMOND
DOG
COLLAR

MARTHA FREEMAN

Holiday House / New York

Art on page 50 by Clement Goodman

Library of Congress Cataloging-in-Publication Data

Freeman, Martha, 1956-
The case of the diamond dog collar / Martha Freeman. — 1st ed.
p. cm. — (A first kids mystery ; 2)
Summary: Seven-year-old Tessa and ten-year-old Cammie, the first female president's
daughters, investigate when a diamond goes missing from the collar of their very
rambunctious dog.
ISBN 978-0-8234-2337-8 (hardcover)
1. White House (Washington, D.C.)—Juvenile fiction.   [1. White House
(Washington, D.C.)—Fiction.   2. Presidents—Family—Fiction.   3. Sisters—
Fiction.   4. Dogs—Fiction.   5. Lost and found possessions—Fiction.
6. Washington (D.C.)—Fiction.   7. Mystery and detective stories.]   I. Title.
PZ7.F87496Cas 2010
[Fic]—dc22
2011005019

ISBN 978-0-8234-2642-3 (paperback)

For my mother,
Barbara Parks Freeman

THE CASE OF THE
DIAMOND
DOG
COLLAR

CHAPTER ONE

MY sister, Tessa, ran into our bedroom yelling: "One of the big, fat diamonds is missing!"

I didn't look up.

Tessa waved her arms to get my attention. "I'm serious, Cammie!"

There are not that many big, fat diamonds in my life, so most likely Tessa was talking about one from our dog's new collar. It had come the day before yesterday, a present from Empress Pu-Chi. She's not a real empress, she's a dog, and she belongs to the president of a nearby nation.

I sighed and closed my book. "They're big, fat, *fake* diamonds, Tessa."

"I know, I know, I know," Tessa said. "But anyway, one of 'em's missing, and you gotta come see."

Have I mentioned my sister is a drama queen?

Still, when she grabbed my arm, I went with her. I didn't have anything better to do. It was Friday afternoon, the start of our March break. Right about now my family was supposed to be on Air Force One flying to California. Only at the last minute, my mom was too busy working on the energy bill to leave Washington.

We didn't want to go to California without Mom.

Since January, when she got to be president of the United States, Tessa and I don't get to see her that much.

Tessa pulled me out the bedroom door and headed for the West Sitting Hall, which is kind of like our living room. Our dog, Hooligan, was there, dozing in his old bed. I was surprised to see him. Usually about now Mr. Bryant would be taking him for his afternoon walk on the South Lawn.

Tessa let go of me and ran over to Hooligan. "Look!" She pointed at the collar, which was bright red, with twelve big, fat, fake diamonds all around it.

Make that eleven.

Hooligan must've heard us because he stretched his paws and opened one eye.

"We should find that missing diamond, Cammie," Tessa said. "It looked real to me. I bet the letter's wrong."

Tessa meant the letter that came with the present. Here is what it said:

Greetings to Hooligan, Esteemed Dog of the First Children of the United States of America,

On behalf of my master, President Manfred Alfredo-Chin, democratically elected leader of a certain nation nearby to your own, I am pleased to offer you the gift of this canine accessory. Please accept it as a token of our admiration and respect, as well as evidence that President Alfredo-Chin bears you no hard feelings for the unfortunate incident earlier this year.

While President Alfredo-Chin's own dog (me!) is practically perfect in every way, he wisely recognizes that in most cases, dogs will be dogs.

> *Supreme Regards,*
> *Empress Pu-Chi*
> *Pekingese*

P.S.—In keeping with the laws on gifts to the pets of presidents, the stones adorning the accessory are not genuine diamonds but attractive facsimiles.

Tessa and I didn't know the word *facsimile*, but our Cousin Nathan did. He is ten like me and lives with us here in the White House along with his mom, my aunt Jen. According to Nathan, *facsimile* is pronounced *fak-si-mi-lee*, and it means "copy"—in other words, fake.

Also, I should explain that when President Manfred Alfredo-Chin visited earlier this year, Hooligan did something that almost caused an international incident. I was glad to know there were no hard feelings.

"What do you mean you think the letter's wrong?" I asked Tessa. "You think someone's lying about the diamonds?"

Tessa shrugged. "All I'm sayin' is they look pretty sparkly."

Hooligan opened his other eye and wiggled his ears. At the same time, I heard canary hysteria from the second-floor kitchen.

"What is wrong with Granny's new—?" Tessa started to ask, but before she could finish, Hooligan jumped like a string had yanked him.

"Hooligan?" I made my voice all calm and soothing. "Be good now."

Hooligan cocked his head as if I had made an excellent suggestion, one worth thinking about...but not right now. Right now he was too busy...

...going *crazy!*

He does this sometimes: lunges forward, thumps his paws, springs high in the air and spins so fast he turns blurry.

"*Catch him!*" I yelled.

Tessa dived, but too soon, and Hooligan, long tail flying, made a neat leap over her and ran like he'd seen rabbits in the distance.

Twee-twee-twee! came from the kitchen, and then the clatter of canary wings against the cage.

Distracted, I turned and didn't see Tessa's body, which I kicked—"*Ow, Cammie!*"—before falling over onto the floor. Lying there, I heard a squeal from down the hall. Then there was an *oof*, a *thump*, a pause and a *thwack.*

Oof and *thump* mean Hooligan's crashed into someone and knocked 'em over. This happens a lot.

But *thwack*? What did that mean?

Twee-twee-twee!

And then: *Aah-rooo!*

Hooligan had started to howl.

Tessa and I untangled, scrambled and ran.

In the center hall, we found a body.

"Are you okay, Mrs. Hedges?" Tessa asked.

She was lying on her back with her eyes closed. Her hands clasped a feather duster to her chest.

"Go away." Mrs. Hedges is one of the maids. She is usually grumpy.

"Hooligan's not really bad," I explained. "He just has—"

"—too much energy. I know." Mrs. Hedges did not open her eyes. "Don't worry about me. I'll just lie here till my strength returns."

"What if it doesn't?" Tessa asked.

"Then someone will cart me away."

Aah-rooo!

"We'll be back!" I told Mrs. Hedges.

We found Hooligan outside the Lincoln Bedroom, singing to the ceiling. High up on the closed door were the unmistakable marks of doggy toenails. Hooligan must've leaped at the door—*thwack*.

"*Hooligan! Be QUIET!!*" Tessa yelled.

This had no effect.

Then the door opened.

A beautiful blonde woman stood there. She was dressed all in white except for a gold necklace and gold earrings. She was smiling...luckily. "Why, Hooligan, shouldn't you be out walking? Hello, Cameron. Hello, Tessa. *Oh!*"

The "*oh!*" was Hooligan pushing past her into the bedroom.

"Hello, Ms. Kootoor," Tessa said. "Sorry about—"

"Never mind, Tessa," said Ms. Kootoor. "You know how I love dogs. Be with you in a moment." The door closed.

Ms. Madeline Kootoor is a friend of my mom's from high school. She used to be a supermodel, then she married somebody rich, then he died. She's been staying with us for a week. According to Dad, we can't throw her out because she raised so much money for my mom's campaign. Plus she and Tessa get along great. They talk about clothes and purses and junk.

The door opened again. Ms. Kootoor came out, holding Hooligan by the collar. At the same time, Mr. Bryant walked up behind us.

Hooligan was thrilled to see Mr. Bryant. He wagged his tail, smiled a big doggy smile and lunged—pulling Ms. Kootoor right over on her face.

"Hooligan!" Mr. Bryant is usually patient, but now he was angry. "Can't a man grab a cup of coffee without all be-whatz-it breaking loose?"

Hooligan finally figured out he was in trouble and dropped to the floor with his paws over his ears. For a moment, he and Ms. Kootoor were lying side by side. Then Ms. Kootoor pushed herself up on her elbows, squinched her eyes, and shook her head.

"Are you okay?" Tessa asked.

Ms. Kootoor tried to smile, but her lipstick was smeared, so the smile came out crooked. 'Nothing a mirror won't fix," she said bravely, "and maybe some aspirin."

From down the hall we could still hear Granny's canary: *Twee-twee-twee!*

CHAPTER TWO

WITH things under control outside the Lincoln Bedroom, Tessa and I went back to check on Mrs. Hedges. She was gone.

Did her strength return? Or was she carted away?

To find out, we decided to go with Mr. Bryant and Hooligan on their walk. On the way to the South Lawn, we could stop and ask Mr. Ross if Mrs. Hedges was all right. Mr. Ross is the chief usher, in charge of taking care of the White House.

We found him in his office on the state floor, also known as the first floor. We live mostly on the second floor.

"She's a little shaken up but otherwise fine." Mr. Ross looked at Mr. Bryant. "I thought Hooligan was supposed to be supervised?"

After Hooligan caused the almost international incident, some changes were made in the White House. Like Hooligan has his very own bedroom where he goes to bed in his crate at nine every night. Also,

Mr. Bryant, who used to run the presidential elevator, got the job of taking care of Hooligan from morning till dinnertime every weekday. On weekends, there's a new guy, Mr. Ng, which is pronounced *ing*. He is from Vietnam. At night, the family—meaning me, Tessa, Granny, Nate and Dad when he's in town—take care of Hooligan till bedtime.

"I left Hooligan napping in his old bed in the West Sitting Hall so I could get a cup of coffee," Mr. Bryant said. "Until yesterday, he'd been behaving so much better. I didn't expect any—"

"Hmm," said Mr. Ross. And he wasn't smiling.

The White House South Lawn is like the biggest backyard ever. During a war a long time ago, a president kept sheep here so he could save money on mowing. Now, there's a swing set and a fountain and a putting green. There are mini forests of trees, a vegetable garden and a basketball court. There is a hidden garden that has paving stones with the hand prints of presidents' kids and grandkids from long ago.

There is also a swimming pool, but we can't use it till the weather gets warm enough.

It was a cool, clear March day. I was wearing a sweatshirt, but Tessa had refused to put one on. She said she didn't have one the right color to go with her outfit. To keep warm, she started to bounce up and down, which made Hooligan hyper all over again. As soon as Mr. Bryant unbuckled the leash, he took off, sprinting in circles.

Mr. Bryant looked down at us. "He had been doing better, hadn't he?"

"Up till yesterday," I agreed.

By now I guess you're wondering about yesterday. Short version: Hooligan broke his leash, and because of that, my sister, a bunch of marines, half the Secret Service and the vice president of the United States almost got blown to Kansas in a helicopter hurricane!

Long version: After school, Nate, Mr. Bryant and Hooligan, Tessa and I had been standing under the awning outside the Diplomatic Reception Room waiting for my dad's helicopter to land.

When anyone in our family travels in a helicopter, a couple of extra ones go along, too, to fool bad guys. So three helicopters were descending toward the landing pad when some birds burst out yakking, and Hooligan went so crazy he busted his leash and raced right toward the spinning blades!

Tessa ran after him. I closed my eyes. The Secret Service agents yelled into their headsets: "South Lawn emergency. Fireball in danger! Repeat, Fireball in danger!"

Fireball is the Secret Service code name for Tessa. Mine is...well, never mind what mine is. For our family, they all have to start with *F*.

Anyway, to avoid squashing anybody, the pilots kept their helicopters hovering in the air, and the blades acted like giant fans. When I opened my eyes, it looked like a massive game of wind-whipped tag, one that turned into hide-and-seek when Hooligan got himself lost in the trees by the tennis court.

Meanwhile, the vice president had been working with his staff in the West Wing. When he saw all the excitement, he came out through the Rose Garden to help.

The scene was frantic and confused with people running every which way, and for a few minutes I couldn't see Hooligan at all. Finally, he reappeared sprinting toward us on the driveway, and that's when Mr. Bryant cut him off.

"How come his paws were so muddy?" I asked Mr. Bryant now. "It's not like it rained this week."

"With the dry spell we're having, the gardeners had been watering," said Mr. Bryant. "I had mud on my shoes, too."

One thing about living in the White House, there are always news guys around, which is why every dinky thing ends up on TV. I mean, sure, my dog and my sister and the vice president and the marines and the Secret Service almost got mixed-up in a helicopter crash in the White House backyard...but is that supposed to be news?

Anyway, the helicopters finally landed, and my mom came over from the Oval Office to meet my dad—same as she does every week.

By then, Ms. Kootoor had joined us under the awning. The news guys love Ms. Kootoor. Dad calls her "cameraman catnip." When she air kissed my dad, their cameras clicked and whirred.

"Whatever was all the fuss, girls?" she asked Tessa and me.

When Tessa explained, Ms. Kootoor laughed her tinkly laugh. Then she knelt and spoke to Hooligan. "Silly puppy. Didn't anyone ever teach you not to chase helicopters?"

Hooligan smiled a big doggy smile and licked her face. He had forgotten all about being in trouble.

CHAPTER THREE

MR. BRYANT, Tessa, Hooligan and I were on our way back upstairs when we ran into Aunt Jen. Her job is being White House hostess, which is like First Lady now when there's a woman president.

Aunt Jen was walking with a skinny, black-haired man. He looked kind of familiar, but what I noticed most were his clothes—jeans, red plaid shirt, cowboy boots. Usually, everyone in the White House except my family is wearing a marine uniform or business clothes. This man looked out of place.

"Just the people, and the dog, I wanted to see," said Aunt Jen. "I'd like to introduce—"

Tessa interrupted. "*Oh my gosh!*" Her eyes were huge. "You're Julius Mormora! Star of Canine Class on TV!"

"Indeed I am, Miss Tessa Parks," said the man. "And this would be your sister, Cameron?"

I was so surprised I answered automatically. "How do you do?"

"I am *fabulous*, as always," said Julius Mormora, and then he spoke to Hooligan. "How are you, my new friend? Ready for Canine Class, I hope?"

Like us, Hooligan was awestruck. He sat right down and put out his paw.

"*Whoa*," I said. "He never did that before."

"Usually with new people," Tessa explained, "he knocks them over and slobbers."

"Mr. Mormora has come for a week to teach Canine Class," Aunt Jen said. "We all recognize, I'm sure, that Hooligan's behavior still needs a little, er . . . tweaking."

Mr. Bryant said, "Hmmph."

Aunt Jen said, "Mr. Mormora, meet Mr. Bryant. He takes care of Hooligan."

Mr. Mormora offered his hand.

Mr. Bryant hesitated before he shook. "If you don't count yesterday," he said, "Hooligan's behavior has improved."

Aunt Jen didn't look convinced. "We're lucky Mr. Mormora's schedule would accommodate us. In fact, he has already been here to tour the house and grounds."

"It was yesterday afternoon that I happened to visit," said Mr. Mormora. "I would have met you then, but there was that incident—"

"—It really wasn't Hooligan's fault," Tessa said.

"Oh?" said Mr. Mormora.

Tessa shook her head. "He never did anything like it before."

"Never ran away before?" asked Mr. Mormora. "Or never broke his leash?"

"Actually, he does that stuff all the time," Tessa said.

"Never, was, uh…chased by so many people before?" asked Mr. Mormora.

"Not in at least a week," I said.

"So what is it exactly that he has never done?" asked Mr. Mormora.

"Never tried to catch helicopters," Tessa said.

"I see," said Mr. Mormora. "Well, we will work on resolving all undesirable behaviors—starting tomorrow when I meet my students."

"We've invited several members of the staff to bring their puppies and participate," said Aunt Jen. "In fact, Mr. Bryant, I believe you have a couple of puppies yourself. Would you like to bring one for Canine Class?"

"We begin promptly at eight a.m.," said Mr. Mormora. "And after that, eight a.m. each day through Wednesday—five days in all."

"But Hooligan likes to sleep in!" Tessa protested.

Mr. Mormora shook his head. "No, no, no! Regular hours and regular habits. This is the way of the Canine Class."

This is also the way of Aunt Jen. No wonder she had invited Mr. Mormora. "Because of the early start," she said, "Mr. Mormora is staying with us in the White House. He'll be joining us for dinner this evening, too."

"Downstairs?" asked Tessa. "*Sweet!*"

Most nights we eat with the family in the second-floor dining room next to our own kitchen. Getting to eat downstairs is a treat.

Mr. Mormora put his hand over his heart. "I came to

this country as a young child. For my first job, I cleaned dog kennels. It is beyond my dreams to be a guest in the White House."

I looked around. We were standing in the center hall on the ground floor. It has cream-colored, arched ceilings, statues of the heads of important dead people, and paintings of kind, smiling first ladies. Now that my family has lived here a few months, I am getting used to the whole White House deal. But Mr. Mormora reminded me it's special.

Mr. Bryant looked at his watch. "Would you mind taking Hooligan back upstairs, girls? I have an engagement this evening."

I took Hooligan's leash and said, "see you at dinner," to Aunt Jen and Mr. Mormora. Then Tessa and I started back upstairs. On the way, Tessa asked, "What's engagement?"

"Date," I said.

Tessa looked confused. "Isn't Mr. Bryant too old for that stuff?"

Sometimes it's my job to educate my sister. "There's lotsa kinds of dates, Tessa. I bet it's only with his daughter—the grown-up one who's always broke."

Back upstairs, we saw there was still time before dinner, so we decided to study Hooligan's collar for clues. The diamonds that were left were each attached with eight silver prongs. Looking closely, we saw four of the prongs for the missing diamond were bent back, and the other four had broken.

"I don't think there's any mystery, Tessa," I said. "I think Hooligan caught his collar on a bush when he was running yesterday, and the diamond got yanked off."

Tessa looked at me and sighed. "Well, *that* would be disappointing."

CHAPTER FOUR

DINNER was pink fish with green-speckled sauce. Mom was delayed—this happens a lot—and Granny had gone out. So it was Dad, Ms. Kootoor, Mr. Mormora, Aunt Jen, Nate, Tessa and me around the table. Tessa, Aunt Jen and Ms. Kootoor talked about fashion. Ms. Kootoor owns this big plaid purse with buckles that to me looks like a big plaid purse with buckles. But according to Tessa and Aunt Jen, it's a Blueberry Bag, and that makes it just about the coolest thing ever. Tessa's Fashionista Barbie even has a teeny tiny one of her own.

"I don't get it," I said. "If it's a 'Blueberry Bag,' why is it plaid?"

"Blueberry is the designer label," said Ms. Kootoor.

"Oh," I said. "And it's special because...?"

Ms. Kootoor gave me a look like I was crazy. "The *style!*"

Tessa leaned toward me and whispered, "Also, it cost a *ton.*"

For dessert we had strawberries with lemon ice.

That's what we were eating when Mom finally came in. She was dressed in her Madam President clothes—blue skirt and jacket, stockings and high heels. She looked tired. After kissing Dad on the cheek, she turned to Mr. Mormora. "A pleasure to meet you." She gave him her hand. "I'm so sorry I couldn't be here earlier, but there's a senator behaving badly, and then that typhoon in Asia..."

Mr. Mormora shook his head. "Sometimes I am glad all I must worry about are dogs."

"Helping people and pets live in harmony is important," said Mom.

"We could use a little more harmony around here," said Aunt Jen.

"My methods are very effective," said Mr. Mormora. Then he told us about some dogs he had met, like a Rottweiler that dug up flowers but only red petunias, and a poodle that ate whole rolls of toilet paper.

Honestly? None of them sounded as bad...I mean as full of energy...as Hooligan.

"I, for one, like Hooligan the way he is," said Ms. Kootoor.

"Oh, please do not mistake me," said Mr. Mormora. "I like all dogs. That is...all dogs except one."

"Which one?" Tessa asked.

Mr. Mormora frowned. "A certain Pekingese dog of my unlucky acquaintance."

"I only ever heard of one Pekingese dog," said Tessa, "the one who sent Hooligan his diamond dog collar, Empress Pu-Chi."

Mr. Mormora dropped his spoon. "But this is the dog to whom I refer!"

"She's not like a close personal friend," I said quickly. "We never even met her."

"Still, the collar is cool," said Tessa. "And guess what?" She paused dramatically. "*One of the diamonds is missing!*"

Tessa was hoping for a big reaction.

But she didn't get it.

Ms. Kootoor took a dainty bite of dessert. "They're only rhinestones, I believe?"

"A rhinestone is the same as a diamond fac-si-mi-le," said Nate.

"But what if they're *not*?" said Tessa. "What if there's a diamond thief loose right here in the White House?"

For a second we all looked around, like, Which one's the thief?

Then Aunt Jen laughed. "I think someone's imagination is running away with her. But tell us, Mr. Mormora, how do you know this Empress Pu-Chi?"

"I have family in that nearby nation," he said. "And a few years ago I was hired to train the animal. The training did not, shall we say, go well."

"Are Pekingese generally difficult?" Dad asked.

Mr. Mormora shook his head. "It is not the breed but only this particular dog. She is very spoiled." Mr. Mormora turned to Mom. "What do you think, Madam President, of Manfred Alfredo-Chin's leadership?"

Mom smiled at Mr. Mormora, took a sip of coffee,

then set down the cup. "I'm so sorry. I have a briefing that begins"—she looked at her watch—"five minutes ago. So if you'll excuse me...."

"*Mo-o-o-om!?*" Tessa whined. "Don't go! What about Monopoly?"

Friday night Monopoly is a tradition in our family. But sometimes Mom's too busy. "You don't need me tonight," Mom said. "You've got plenty of players! Later I'll be up to give you a kiss."

CHAPTER FIVE

MS. KOOTOOR took Mom's place at Monopoly, and you never saw anyone go bankrupt so fast! Only a half hour into the game, she landed on Boardwalk and couldn't pay the rent.

We were up in the Solarium, which is like our family room. It's on the third floor, and, at night when the monuments on the Mall are lit, the view is beautiful. Besides me and Ms. Kootoor, Tessa, Dad and Nate were playing. Mr. Mormora was preparing for his class in the morning. Aunt Jen doesn't like games.

When Nate won, he punched the air. "Loser puts the game away! Loser puts the game away!"

Ms. Kootoor raised her hand. "That would be me."

Nate looked embarrassed. "Oh...but you don't count."

"Because you're a guest," Tessa said. "Anyway, Cammie doesn't mind."

I said, "*Me?!*"

Ms. Kootoor shook her head. "No, no, Cameron. Let me. I lost fair and square."

Granny came in while Ms. Kootoor was collecting the pieces.

"Past your bedtime, isn't it, Judge?" Dad said.

Granny laughed. "I'm wide awake! Must be that splash of coffee late in the day."

"Maybe some news will lull you to sleep," Dad said. He punched the remote . . . and you'll never guess what picture came on the screen: a big, fat diamond!

Tessa squealed.

". . . missing from the National Museum of a certain nearby nation, Jan. Officials are calling the sixty-karat stone known as El Brillante an 'irreplaceable national treasure.'" It was Larry who was talking. He and pretty, blonde Jan do the local news we always watch.

Now there was a close-up of Jan, who looked concerned. "And the gem was kept in a sealed vault, Larry?"

"Locked up tight, Jan." Larry looked concerned, too. "The theft was discovered this morning, but authorities say it's possible the diamond had been missing for as long as a month."

Tessa said, "*See!* I told you a diamond was missing!"

Nate said, "Earth to Tessa. Different diamond."

Tessa shook her head. "But it's the exact same nearby nation! There's gotta be a connection."

"I don't see how," Dad said. "El Brillante is one of the largest diamonds in the world. Even if Hooligan's was real—by comparison, it's puny."

Tessa was offended. *"Puny?"*

"And besides," Dad said. "That diamond was missing from a vault a thousand miles away. The fake stone is missing from Hooligan's collar."

Behind me, Granny cleared her throat. "If anyone is interested," she said, "I think Tessa has a point."

Before she was a judge, Granny was a police officer, so she is the only one in the family with actual crime-fighting experience. Dad, Nate and Ms. Kootoor tried to argue with her, but she wouldn't budge.

"It's like I told the girls last time they were detecting," she said. "Something illogical just might be a clue. This time, the incidents may seem unrelated, but happening together like that? An unlikely coincidence."

CHAPTER SIX

WHEN Mom came in to say good night, she was wearing an old gray Stanford hoodie and pink plaid pajama bottoms.

Tessa groaned. "*Mo-o-o-om!* I don't get how you and Ms. Kootoor ever even got to be friends. She is so stylish! Like that Blueberry Bag—"

"What's a Blueberry Bag?" Mom asked.

I put my hands over my ears. "If I hear 'Blueberry Bag' one more time, I will scream."

Tessa shrugged. "We can talk about diamonds instead. Did you hear one is missing from a certain nearby nation, Mom? It's called El Brillante! And you wanna know what I think?"

Mom nodded and yawned. "Uh-huh, muffin. What do you think?"

"It's got something to do with the diamond missing from Hooligan's collar!"

"Uh-huh," said Mom. "Interesting."

"You should tell the FBI that, Mom. They will want to know," said Tessa.

"Uh . . . okay. But first, let's see what develops," Mom said.

Tessa crossed her arms over her chest. "Well, if *that's* your attitude, then me and Cammie will investigate ourselves."

"Cammie and *I*," said Mom.

"Great!" said Tessa. "We could definitely use your help."

"Oh, dear, muffin, I didn't mean . . ." Mom tried to tell Tessa she was only correcting her English.

But Tessa wasn't listening. She was too busy planning our investigation. "First, we interview witnesses," she said. "I know—how about President Manfred Alfredo-Chin? One thing I want to know is who really wrote the letter from Empress Pu-Chi. Is he sure those diamonds on the collar aren't real? After that—"

"Muffin?" Mom interrupted. "It really wouldn't do for you to phone the president of another country and ask questions. The secretary of state would have a fit. But I do have an idea. If you're interested in diamonds, one of the most famous in the world is right here at the Smithsonian Museum of Natural History. It's called the Hope Diamond. What if you and your sister and Nate go see it this week? It's not a trip to California, but at least it's a project."

"Can you come with us?" Tessa asked.

Mom hesitated. When she used to be a plain old senator from California, we could do regular things like go to the mall or the zoo. Now that she's president, there has to be loads of security anytime anyone in the family goes anyplace—even school. For Mom, if she even takes a walk, they shut down streets and surround her with officers and motorcycles.

I bet she wanted to come with us, but the hassle would never be worth it. "I'm sorry, girls," she said. "But Granny would love to go."

Tessa rubbed her eyes and sniffed like she was going to cry, but really she was just being dramatic. I know because as soon as Mom kissed us, said good night and closed the door, she was totally fine again. "Cammie?" she whispered. "You agree with me about the missing diamond, right?"

"Wrong," I said.

"Oh," said Tessa. "Well, okay. But you'll still help me investigate?"

"I guess," I said.

"Because you don't have anything better to do?"

"Right," I said. And I closed my eyes. And I know this sounds weird, but I think I heard my little sister smiling.

CHAPTER SEVEN

THE next morning arrived with Granny at seven a.m. "Rise and shine, girls! Canine Class today!"

Tessa pulled up the covers and grumbled, "I already know 'sit' and 'stay.'"

"Me, too. I can even roll over." I demonstrated.

Granny laughed but there's never any point in arguing with her. Ten minutes later we were dressed and brushed and ready to name the canary. He lives in a cage in our family's kitchen and belongs to Granny, but she won't tell us where he came from.

It's a minor mystery.

That day it was Tessa's turn, and she tried "Sunny."

"Because he's yellow," she explained.

"*Boring.*" I said.

"I have to agree," Granny said. "Nate's turn tomorrow—if he gets up in time."

So far, my cousin still hadn't come down from his bedroom on the third floor. No surprise. He may know everything, but he's so lazy he's always missing breakfast.

Tessa and I sat down at the table. I barely had my napkin in my lap when she crossed her arms over her chest. "We already found something illogical," she said. "So next we interview witnesses."

I shook my head. "Huh?"

Tessa pointed at the pink baseball cap on her head. "*Duh*, Cammie!"

It took a second, but then I got it. The pink cap is what she wears for detecting.

"You mean two missing diamonds at the same time is illogical," I said. "But we don't know for sure that Hooligan's was even stolen. So what if first we look around and see if we can find it?"

This was the most obvious idea ever, but Tessa nodded like I had said something smart. "That could work. But where do we look?"

"Good morning!" Ms. Kootoor was standing in the kitchen doorway. "Here—let me take those." She took bowls of cereal from Granny and brought them to us at the table. "Did I hear you girls say you're looking for something?"

"The diamond!" Tessa said.

"Ah." Ms. Kootoor nodded. 'And where do you think it might be?"

I explained about the bent and broken prongs. "We think it came off yesterday when Hooligan was being chased."

"So here's the plan," said Tessa. "We'll start looking in the shrubs and trees on the South Lawn—right after Canine Class."

A few minutes later, we ran into Mr. Mormora and Aunt Jen's secretary, Mrs. Crowe, in the Dip Room.

"Oh my goodness!" said Mr. Mormora when we stepped out under the awning. "The backyard is enormous!"

Mrs. Crowe laughed. "You haven't been out to the South Lawn yet?"

He shook his head. "I have not had the chance. I believe everything has been made ready for us, though?"

"Follow me," said Mrs. Crowe.

The class was going to be held on the grass in the middle of the driveway—the same place the helicopters land.

To my surprise, Nate was already there waiting.

And guess who else?

Puppies!

Big ones, small ones, all different breeds plus mutts—but here's the thing: They were all around six months old...and Hooligan is two *years* old! When Mr. Ng brought him out a few minutes later, Hooligan looked big and goofy—like a fifth grader repeating kindergarten.

Hooligan wasn't embarrassed, though. Dragging Mr. Ng by the leash, he charged right in, bumping the little guys with his nose and rolling them over to get a good sniff. Soon there was a spiderweb of leashes, and Mr. Ng and the rest of the humans were going over and under to sort things out.

It took a while, but eventually Hooligan's leash was attached only to Hooligan. That's when Mr. Ng came over and handed it to me. "Good luck, Cameron," he said.

Mr. Ng is tall and skinny and kind of serious. Mr. Bryant says he's shy, but he makes me a little nervous.

Now—and it wasn't his fault—he made me a lot nervous. "What?!" I said.

Mr. Ng shrugged. "Somebody's got to be the Canine Buddy. Your dad talked to me about it, and..."

I took the leash but immediately held it out to Tessa. "Don't you wanna—?"

Tessa put her hands behind her back. "No, no, no, Cammie! You're the responsible older sister."

"Nate?" I tried. But that was hopeless. He's into piano, not pets.

Mr. Mormora was calling the class to order when the last puppy pupil arrived, a black puffball mutt, along with his owner, Mr. Bryant. Of course, Hooligan was thrilled to see Mr. Bryant! He lunged and would've pulled me over, but I leaned back with every ounce I own. *"Hooligan! Stay!"*

Too bad he actually did, which I never expected. Unbalanced, I sat down on a cockapoo. The cockapoo wasn't hurt, but he snapped at me, which made the owner squeal and Hooligan growl. This got the rest of the dogs excited, and we were on the verge of total puppy upset when Mr. Mormora dropped to dog's-eye level and spoke: *"Amigos, perros,* dogs of my heart..."

And like magic, every pup was quiet.

In Canine Class, the people are known as Canine Buddies, CBs for short, and the dogs are Canines in Training, or CITs. To start with, we all went around in a circle and introduced ourselves.

Hooligan and I were first, and then the woman next to me with the cockapoo. "I'm Ann Major. I'm an assistant press secretary to President Parks. And this is my dog, Pickles."

After that, nine more Canine Buddies introduced themselves and their CITs. There was a poodle, four golden retrievers, a labradoodle, a Chihuahua and two I'm-not-sure-whats. Last was Mr. Bryant. He is always very dignified.

"I am Mr. Willis Bryant," he said, "and this is my canine, Cottonball."

In case you have never seen Canine Class on TV, this is how it goes: Mr. Mormora takes one of the CITs as an example and gives him a command—like "sit."

The dog sits. This could be a mean dog or a dumb dog or a dog that speaks Chinese, it doesn't matter. The dog sits. No one knows how Mr. Mormora does this, but he does.

That day, all the other dogs and their trainers watched Mr. Mormora convince a CIT golden retriever to sit several different times from several different angles. Then he turned toward the rest of us. "All right, Canine Buddies, it is now your turn. Please, command your CITs to sit."

Instead of watching the golden retriever, Hooligan had been making friends with a Chihuahua. I did not have a good feeling. But I stood up straight like Mr. Mormora did, and I tried to copy the way he talks: "Hooligan—*sit*."

Hooligan didn't move. Pickles scratched herself, and the I'm-not-sure-what on our left tried to dig a hole. Only a poodle and Mr. Bryant's dog, Cottonball, actually sat.

Then . . . so did Hooligan.

It was a miracle! From where the spectators were standing, I heard Tessa squeal. When I looked over, I noticed a whole bunch of cameras were aimed at Hooligan. The press loves him almost as much as they love Ms. Kootoor.

After that, all the CITs tried sitting again. And again. And Hooligan sat every time! Later, when we tried "stay," he did that every time, too.

Canine Class only lasts forty-five minutes because, as Mr. Mormora explained it, "canine concentration is not powerful." Even so, there's some waiting around, so I asked Ms. Major about being an assistant press secretary. She told me she used to be a TV reporter, but then she went to work for my mom's campaign. Now her job is mostly keeping track of what's written and broadcast about our family, and Hooligan, too.

The end of Canine Class is always the same. Mr. Mormora thanks everyone for participating and gives out Canine Cookies. They are the shape of ordinary dog biscuits, but they have red and yellow stripes.

"You see how it is that Hooligan is a star pupil?" said Mr. Mormora. "It is the positive peer pressure. With the younger dogs, he wants to be a leader."

I hadn't noticed Ms. Kootoor with the other spectators, but now she was walking toward us with Dad and Tessa. "Great job, puppy!" she said, and scratched him behind the ears. He nosed her hand and whined.

Then Mr. Bryant came up, pulled along by Cottonball.

"Sit!" said Mr. Bryant. Cottonball looked at him, trying to remember what that word meant.

Tessa said, "Like this," and sat down on the grass. Cottonball didn't copy her, he tackled her! Then Hooligan piled on.

Mr. Bryant and I were trying to pull them off when Mr. Mormora spoke: "Gentlemen?"

Right away the dogs backed off and sat down.

Tessa wasn't hurt—unless dog slobber hurts. She wiped her face and asked Mr. Mormora, "How do you *do* that?"

He smiled. "It is just having the confidence. Dogs respect confidence. By the time we hold graduation on Wednesday, each of these dogs will be a fine example of Canine Class, and one will be Top Dog—the number one student. That dog will receive a blue ribbon, and its picture will appear on boxes of Canine Cookies. Hooligan, what do you think? Have you the makings of the Top Dog?"

CHAPTER EIGHT

WHEN Tessa was four, she got a pink Barbie watch for her birthday. She still wears it, even though I tell her she's too old. Now, according to Barbie, it was nine thirty—still early for a Saturday morning. But already Canine Class was over, the puppies were gone, and Tessa, Hooligan and I were riding a mini-tractor past the tennis court on the South Lawn. Behind us on the tractor was a load of very smelly compost.

It was Mr. Golly, one of the groundskeepers, who was giving us a ride. Tessa was next to him in front, and I was on the little bench seat in the back, holding tight to Hooligan. We had been trying to follow his trail from Thursday on foot, and Mr. Golly had picked us up like hitchhikers.

"Your parents won't mind, will they?" he called as the tractor bump-bumped along.

Tessa and I chorused: "No!" because—both of us were thinking—*we will never tell them.*

And if we were lucky, nobody else would tell either.

The thing is, wherever Tessa and I go, we're being watched by the Secret Service. Like right then, I could see two agents: Malik was standing by the fountain in the middle of the lawn, and Jeremy was over to our right on the basketball court. It was the weekend, and they were assigned to the White House residence, so they didn't have to wear suits. Instead they had on khakis and polo shirts, but with their straight posture, short hair and shiny shoes, they still looked like Secret Service.

Mr. Golly's compost was bound for the new kitchen garden near the far fence. The ride down there gave Tessa an excellent opportunity to do some detecting.

"Mr. Golly," she asked, "have you or any of the other groundskeepers seen a big, fat, fake diamond lying around the South Lawn since Wednesday afternoon? Or possibly a big, fat, not-fake diamond?"

Mr. Golly adjusted the brim on his hat. "Hector found an orange flip-flop last week. And we're always finding Frisbees and footballs and kites. I don't remember diamonds, though—fake or not fake. Why are you asking?"

Tessa and I took turns explaining how one was missing.

"If you're looking for clues," said Mr. Golly, "there are plenty of dried footprints in the flowerbeds."

"I don't think footprints will work," I said. "We already know a zillion people were down here—chasing Hooligan and flattening flowers."

Mr. Golly agreed it was a mess. "But a crew and I raked up the dead stuff yesterday."

Tessa and I looked at each other. Had the diamond been raked up, too?

"What happens to the dead stuff?" I asked.

"We grind it for compost," Mr. Golly explained.

"And did you do that already?" Tessa asked.

"Yesterday afternoon," Mr. Golly said.

Sometimes my sister and I don't have to say anything. We just understand: If Hooligan had dropped the diamond in a flowerbed, by now it was diamond dust.

Mr. Golly pulled the tractor up next to the kitchen garden, which was only a big, bare patch of dirt. Later in the spring, vegetables would be planted. Aunt Jen had told Tessa and me we could help.

"Does your dog have any bloodhound in him?" Mr. Golly asked.

"According to Dad, he's got everything," said Tessa.

"So maybe you can get him to track down that diamond," said Mr. Golly.

This seemed worth a try, so, while Mr. Golly scooped compost with a pitchfork, Tessa took Hooligan's leash off and explained the idea to him. Meanwhile, I looked around. The South Lawn is more like a big park than a backyard. Assuming the diamond still existed, how were we ever going to find it?

Tessa stood up. "Okay, he gets it," she said.

"Are you sure?" I asked.

"Totally," said Tessa. "Ready, Hooligan? *Go!*"

Hooligan lunged, thumped, sprang, spun—and then he was off, with Tessa and me sprinting to keep up.

Soon we were in the trees, and sure enough,

Hooligan had his nose to the ground like a vacuum cleaner. I was just thinking this plan could actually work when he stopped dead in his tracks and Tessa, ahead of me, almost tumbled over him.

"Cammie, look!" she said. "He found it!"

CHAPTER NINE

SOMETHING told me that was just too easy.

And something turned out to be right.

I didn't know what it was Hooligan had found in the trees, but it wasn't a diamond.

Dogs don't eat diamonds.

"Bad dog!" I scolded him.

But my sister scratched his ears. "Don't listen, puppy. She doesn't mean it."

"I do, too!" I said.

"Maybe I didn't explain it to him right." Tessa unbuckled his collar and held it up so he could see the space where the diamond used to be. "That's what you're looking for, puppy," she said. "Okay?" She buckled the collar back on. "Ready, set—find that diamond!"

Have I mentioned Hooligan has too much energy?

First he led us over by the west fence, then we ran up past the pool, across the driveway and around the putting green twice before we cut south again. I play midfield on the D.C. Destoyers soccer team, but even so I was out of breath. The only reason I kept up at all was that he kept pausing and gobbling junk—probably crucial pieces of evidence.

It was a warm day for March, and I was getting sweaty when Hooligan solved that problem—he ran through the fountain, so of course Tessa and I did, too. If we weren't already in trouble for riding the tractor with Mr. Golly, we for sure were in trouble now, but there was no time to worry about that. Hooligan was bee-lining for the kitchen garden—right back where we started.

"Watch out!" I yelled to Mr. Golly. He was forking up the last smelly scoop and didn't see Hooligan, who sideswiped him—*ka-bam!*

"Are you all right?" I asked when we got to him.

"Are you mad?" Tessa asked.

Before Mr. Golly could answer, Jeremy and Malik appeared. Jeremy is a really big guy with a deep voice. Malik is my second-favorite Secret Service agent after Charlotte. They had seen the whole thing.

Now Malik reached out a hand to help Mr. Golly, and Jeremy asked, "You okay there?"

Mr. Golly was wiping compost from his eyes. He said, "Reckon I'll live," and shook his head. Black bits flew out of his hair.

"I think we should escort you girls back to the house," Malik said. "You're going to want to get out of your wet shoes and socks."

"Mr. Ng will be here for Hooligan shortly," said Jeremy.

Tessa had grabbed Hooligan's leash and run over to where he lay in the shade. Now she called me over, too. "Look," she said and pointed at the fur around his snout. There was plenty of plain brown dirt. But there was something else besides—a whole lot of crumbs, bright red and bright yellow.

Only one thing leaves red and yellow crumbs.

"Canine Cookies!" I said.

"That must be what he kept stopping to eat," Tessa said. "But who dropped them?"

"Mr. Mormora most likely," I said. "But didn't he tell Mrs. Crowe he'd never been out here? There's no reason he'd lie about that . . . is there?"

CHAPTER TEN

ALL the Secret Service agents wear radio headsets so they can keep in touch. That's why, when we got to the Dip Room door, Granny was waiting with our slippers and frowning.

"Sorry, Granny," Tessa and I chorused.

"Hmmph," said Granny, then she held out our slippers. "Change out of your wet shoes and socks so you don't make a mess or catch pneumonia. After lunch, you'll each write an apology to Mr. Golly."

Oh well. It could've been worse.

On weekends, we eat lunch in the family kitchen. Usually, either Granny or Dad makes it. Granny is better because she takes special orders. Like my sandwich doesn't get mustard, Tessa's doesn't get mayonnaise and Nate doesn't eat anything green, like lettuce.

Dad makes all our sandwiches the same, and if we complain, he says, "How would you like to make *my* lunch for a change?"

Today Granny put plates down for Nate, Tessa and me, then made a surprise announcement: "We're going to go see the Hope Diamond tonight!"

It turned out Mrs. Crowe had phoned the Museum of Natural History, and Saturday at seven p.m. was the best time for our visit. The museum would be closed, so keeping us safe would be easy. Plus we wouldn't be bugging the regular visitors with all the hoo-ha that happens when we go someplace.

"One of the assistant curators, a Mr. Rubio, has agreed to meet us and talk about the diamond," Granny said. "And Ms. Kootoor is coming, too. She's always been fond of diamonds."

"That's for sure," Tessa said. "She's got loads of diamond jewelry, and even a diamond whistle!"

Granny raised her eyebrows. "Why on earth—?"

"Her dad gave it to her," Tessa explained, "when she moved to New York City to get famous. If she's ever in danger, she's supposed to blow the whistle."

"Has she ever used it?" I asked.

Tessa shook her head. "Nope. But she keeps it with her just in case."

Granny nodded. "You know? A safety whistle might be a good idea. But I don't see the point of the diamonds."

Tessa's mouth opened. Luckily, it was empty. "How can you say that, Granny? The diamonds are for style!"

When we had finished our sandwiches, Granny looked at her watch and pushed back her chair. "With this warm weather, I've made a tennis date—the first of the year. Can you entertain yourselves?"

Nate said a friend of his was coming over. They were going to shoot hoops.

Lucky, I thought. All my friends were out of town for March break.

But Tessa said we'd have no problem keeping busy.

"We won't?" I said.

"*Hello-o-o?*" She crossed her arms over her chest. "We've got a mystery to solve? Remember?"

After lunch, we sat down at our desks to write to Mr. Golly. Along with our beds and posters, the desks came with us from our old house. But the rest of the furniture in our room belongs to the White House collection. Aunt Jen helped Tessa and me pick what we wanted. When we leave someday, it will go back in storage—or maybe the new president will have kids that pick the same stuff.

I spent a long time writing. I really did feel bad that Hooligan had knocked Mr. Golly into the compost. It was going to take a lot of shampoo to get the smell out of his hair.

Tessa drew a picture of a man lying down and a brown dog with a frowny face. Over the dog it said: "Sorry!"

When we were done, we folded our notes and put them in envelopes for Granny to address.

Then it was time for detecting.

In the West Sitting Hall, where Hooligan's old wicker dog bed is, there's a comfortable stripe-y sofa that's good for thinking. By now, Mr. Ng had brought Hooligan back inside. After his busy morning, Hooligan was napping. Tessa and I sat down on the sofa, and I wrote down everything we knew about the case so far:

- Hooligan's diamond probably disappeared Thursday during helicopter incident.
- Prongs on collar broken or bent back.
- Acc. to Jan/Larry: El Brillante was missing Friday morning from museum.
- But could have been missing a month.
- Connection between El Brillante and Hooligan's missing diamond?
- Gardeners found flip-flop last week but no diamond this week.
- But did they by mistake grind up diamond?
- Or is it on South Lawn somewhere?
- Canine Cookie crumbs on Hooligan's nose.
- Used to be Canine Cookies all over South Lawn.
- Not anymore.
- Did Mr. Mormora drop them?
- But Mr. Mormora said he hadn't been on South Lawn.

By then, my hand was tired so I shook it out. Tessa had been reading over my shoulder and making suggestions.

"I don't like it if Mr. Mormora lied to us," she said.

"He's nice though," I said. "I like the way he talks to dogs."

"You should write down what he said at dinner, too," Tessa said. Then she dictated:

- Mr. Mormora has family in nearby nation.
- Mr. Mormora doesn't like Empress Pu-Chi.
- Mr. Mormora asked Mom about President Manfred Alfredo-Chin.

"I don't think Mr. Mormora likes President Alfredo-Chin either," she said.

"So what?" I said.

Tessa waved her arms dramatically the way she does. "So I don't know what! But isn't it suspicious?"

"Isn't what suspicious?" Granny had come in from tennis. She was pink and a little sweaty. Hooligan looked up when he heard her voice.

"Do you want to help us do detecting?" Tessa asked.

Granny said sure, and together we read through the notes. We had to explain about the cookies and the diamond maybe being ground up.

"If I were the detective," Granny said thoughtfully, "I'd say the next move was obvious. It's time to interview Mr. Mormora."

CHAPTER ELEVEN

MR. MORMORA was staying in a guest room on the third floor, down the hall from Aunt Jen and Nate. We were going up there when Charlotte came into the West Sitting Hall. Charlotte is my favorite Secret Service agent.

"Mr. Mormora?" Charlotte said when we told her what we were doing. "He's out sightseeing—one of those bus tours."

Tessa dropped back down on the sofa. "Well, *that's* disappointing."

Charlotte said, "Sorry," then she held an envelope out to me. "For you, Cammie."

Tessa and I get letters all the time—not as many as my mom or Hooligan, but too many for us to sort ourselves. First they go to the office that handles White House mail, and most get answered by volunteers. When there's a special letter, we see it after it's checked out by the Secret Service.

"Is it a good one?" I asked.

"You're going to like it," she said and winked.

"What the…?" But then I looked at the address, and instantly forgot about Mr. Mormora, missing diamonds, and even Hooligan. This is what it said:

Camron Parks
The White House
1600 Pensylvania Ave.
Washingtun, DC 20500

Tessa read over my shoulder. "Hey—somebody's as bad a speller as you! So that must mean it's from—"

I sighed. "Paul Song." And I guess my face went moony because Tessa rolled her eyes.

"Oh, brother," she said, "and you make fun of *me* for having crushes!"

Paul Song, in case you don't know, is part of the best band in America, The Song Boys. Not that long ago, he and his brothers played a concert at the White House, and I got to meet him. He was really nice, not stuck up at all.

And now he'd actually written me a letter!

Dear Cammie,

You will probably think I'm a dork for writing you an old-fashon letter with a stamp and everything. But right now we were sitting here in the hotel, and I saw this writting paper and I thought it would be funny to write you.

On TV yesterday I saw how that TV dog guy is staying with you and giving Hooligan dog lessons! That is so cool! I wish he could give my dog dog lessons, too. I miss my dog when we are on tour. Did I tell you about him? He was a puppy at the pound when we picked him, and he grew up to be funny-looking but not as funny-looking as Hooligan. (Don't let Hooligan read that part. JK.) My dog's name is Singalong because when he was a puppy he liked to howl with us.

My brothers don't know it, but Singalong likes me best. That's because I sneak him dog biscuts. I am going to have to stop, though. Or else he will be funny-looking AND fat. Here is a picture:

Okay, so gotta go do the show. After LA, we go to San Fransisco and then Orgon.

See you later. I hope?

Best—Paul Song

PS—If I just wrote "Paul," would you know it was me, or do you know lots of people named Paul?

"It's not a very interesting letter," said Tessa.

"Hey!" I flipped it over and elbowed her. "It's personal!"

"Like a cartoon dog is *so* personal," said Tessa. "He didn't sign it 'love.' And he can't even spell your name."

"You're just jealous," I said.

"Am not."

"Are too."

"Girls?" It was Granny. She had gone to shower and change her clothes. Now she was back. "We need to eat early if we're going to get to the museum on time. Go get yourselves cleaned up, and I believe Aunt Jen has put clothes out."

Pretty much any time we go anywhere, the news guys are there with their cameras. That's why Aunt Jen picks our clothes. If she didn't, I would wear gym shorts, and Tessa would wear pink party dresses.

Usually I don't mind changing, but now I was grumpy after arguing with Tessa. "I look fine already!" I insisted.

Tessa looked me up and down. "You'd at least better fix your hair, Cammie. What if icky old *Paul Song* sees you on TV?"

CHAPTER TWELVE

THE Smithsonian Museum of Natural History is located on the National Mall, less than a mile from our house. So you'd think we could have walked there, right?

Wrong.

To keep us safe, we had to be driven. Tessa, Nate and I went in a van with Charlotte. Granny, Dad and Ms. Kootoor followed in another van.

You're probably thinking: *Lucky-y-y! She gets to have a driver to take her places!*

But sometimes I feel more like I'm trapped. I mean, it would have been nice to walk to the museum with nobody knowing or caring who I was—to be like I used to be, a normal kid.

Of course, back then, I didn't appreciate how normal was nice.

The museum building sits at the top of some big wide steps, and it's full of cool stuff like dinosaur bones, crazy-looking bugs, pretty rocks and stuffed wild animals. Usually, it is also full of people. But when we walked through the big heavy doors, there were only a couple of guards and a man in a suit and tie. That was Mr. Rubio, the assistant curator. With so few people, the museum was kind of spooky and quiet. I felt like I was in church.

Tessa didn't. She tore through the doors, past the stuffed elephant in the lobby and around Mr. Rubio— "Hi, nice to meet you!" Charlotte ran after her, trying to keep up.

The Hope Diamond has its own room on the second floor. Over the doorway is a helpful sign that reads, THE HOPE DIAMOND. It sits on a white velvet pedestal in a glass and metal case. It's more than an inch long, which is big for a diamond, and it's gray-blue, which is the main reason it's special.

Mr. Rubio and the six of us clustered around the case. I got out my notebook, ready to write. Tessa was wearing her pink detecting hat.

"Over the centuries the Hope Diamond has been owned by millionaires, lords, ladies and kings," Mr. Rubio explained.

Nate, who knows everything, said he heard there was a curse.

Mr. Rubio nodded. "The story goes that the diamond was stolen from the eye of a statue of a goddess, and the goddess cursed all future owners."

Uh oh. Were the museum walls going to crumble?

"But there's no evidence for the story at all," Mr. Rubio continued. "What is true is that a lot of people who owned this diamond were unlucky and died broke."

"Well, that's crazy," Tessa said. "If you had this big diamond, you could sell it and not be broke anymore!"

"Sell something so *beautiful?!*" Ms. Kootoor was horrified.

"If the diamond's unlucky," Granny said, "why is it called 'Hope'?"

Mr. Rubio said it was owned by the Hope family in the 1800s, and that was the name that stuck. "The diamond was actually mined in India in the 1600s, then sold to the king of France," he said. "At that time, it was known as the French Blue. Later it disappeared and turned up in London, but by then it was smaller. It had been cut and reshaped."

"I didn't know diamonds were cut more than once," said Granny.

"Oh, yes," Mr. Rubio said. "Sometimes they're recut to eliminate a flaw. Sometimes a particular shape goes out of fashion. Other times, a diamond will be divided into smaller stones."

Dad asked, "What is it that makes a diamond special in the first place?"

"Diamonds are rare," said Mr. Rubio. "It takes billions of years for one to form deep under the surface of the earth. And the pressure makes a diamond one of the hardest materials known."

"But can't they be manufactured?" Dad asked.

"Yes, but the process is as expensive as finding one in nature," said Mr. Rubio. "Of course, there are also diamond facsimiles. They can be made out of all sorts of minerals, or even plastic."

"So how does one tell the difference between real and fake?" Granny asked.

"It's not always easy," Mr. Rubio said. "But I can demonstrate one test. Is anyone wearing a diamond?"

Granny took off her engagement ring and held it out. Mr. Rubio took it, and raised it to his mouth. *"Ewwww!"* said Tessa. "You're not gonna lick it, are you?"

Mr. Rubio opened his mouth like he just might... but he was kidding. Instead, he made his mouth into an O and blew a sharp little puff.

"See that?" he asked us.

"The diamond didn't fog up," Granny said.

Mr. Rubio nodded. "That's because it's real."

"Well, I hope so," said Granny.

"A real diamond has special physical properties that keep it slightly cool at all times," Mr. Rubio said. "That's why an old-fashioned nickname for diamonds is 'ice.' Those same properties mean that a diamond clears condensation almost instantly. A fake typically requires several seconds, or else has to be wiped clean."

Tessa crossed her arms over her chest the way she does when she's interviewing a witness. "Mr. Rubio," she said, "what would happen if a diamond got stuck in a compost grinder?"

Mr. Rubio raised his eyebrows. I don't think anyone had ever asked him that before. "Uh...how big a diamond?" he asked.

Tessa showed him with her fingers.

"I should think a diamond that big would break the

mechanism . . . and probably make a horrible noise, too," he said.

"Write that down, Cammie," Tessa said.

"But the diamond we're looking for is fake," I said.

Tessa sighed and recrossed her arms. "Mr. Rubio," she said, "what would happen if a *fake* diamond got caught in a compost grinder?"

"I'm no expert on fake diamonds," he said. "But I should think it would grind up just fine."

A diamond, even a famous blue one, is only interesting for so long. We looked around at the other things in the room—a meteorite, a crystal and a huge sheet of copper—then at some fancy jewelry in the room next door. It was almost time to go when Nate asked Mr. Rubio, "So how much money is the Hope Diamond worth?"

"*Nate!*" Tessa delivered her best Aunt Jen look. "Money's rude!"

But Mr. Rubio said he didn't mind answering. "You see, the Hope Diamond is worth two things at once: everything and nothing."

"Huh?" said Tessa.

Mr. Rubio explained. "Looked at one way, the Hope Diamond is worth so much money it can't even be calculated. There is not another like it in the universe! But looked at another, it's worth nothing. That's because it's so famous, it couldn't possibly be sold. Any buyer would recognize it and know it had been stolen."

I thought of something. "Is El Brillante the same amount famous?"

"The diamond that disappeared in a certain nearby nation?" said Mr. Rubio. "I would say so, yes."

"So same thing," I said. "No one could sell it. And if that's true—why would anybody steal it?"

Mr. Rubio shrugged and shook his head. "That's one question I can't answer."

CHAPTER THIRTEEN

THAT night it was Dad who came in to give us our kisses.

"Where's Mom?" Tessa asked.

"She's sorry, girls," Dad said. "Something came up."

"Something more important than us?" Tessa said.

"Nothing's more important than you," Dad said. "But some things are more urgent."

"Hmmph," said Tessa. "Hey—did you hear Cammie got a *letter*? From Paul *So-o-o-ong*."

"Aren't there any secrets in this house?" I said.

Dad smiled. "What did the letter say? Or don't you want to tell?"

"I'll tell!" Tessa said. "He can't even spell, and besides that—"

Dad held up his hand. "All right, Tessa. Cammie's entitled to some privacy. But, uh, sweetie...do you think you'll write him back?"

"Maybe," I said. "But not right away. Tessa and I have a mystery to solve."

Tessa woke me before I knew I was asleep.

She was bouncing on my bed. *"Cammie!"*

"Go away."

"No, *seriously*! I thought of something! We have to do some detecting!"

I didn't want to, but I opened my eyes. It was still dark. "What time is it?"

Tessa didn't answer, just pulled me out of bed. A weird dream had woken her. In it, Hooligan's diamond collar was on display in the Hope Diamond's case. Mr. Rubio was there, and he wrote on the foggy glass with his finger "Are they real?"

"Do you get it, Cammie?" Tessa asked.

I shook my head to clear the sleep out. Then... "Oh—you mean the breath test? You want to do it on Hooligan's collar!"

I had to give Tessa credit. Why hadn't I thought of that?

Without another word, we tiptoed out of our room and down the hall. Hooligan's own bedroom is next to the elevator. It's a room some first ladies have used for doing hair and makeup, but a long time ago a president's dog named Millie had her puppies here. Now it's where Hooligan goes to bed in his crate.

Tessa whispered, "You block him in, and I'll get the collar."

Hooligan's crate has a black wire gate at the front. I crouched down, unlatched it and pulled it partway open. Tessa slid her hand in to unbuckle the collar. All the time my heart was pounding.

"Got it!" Tessa whispered.

Hooligan snuffled and shifted, and I thought my heart would stop. We weren't doing anything wrong, but if he woke up, he'd wake the whole house.

Back in our room, I breathed again. Then I turned on the lamp. In the light, the collar seemed extra sparkly, and I couldn't help wondering how much it would be worth if the diamonds were real. Was I holding millions of dollars?

"Your breath or mine?" Tessa asked.

"It was your idea," I said.

Tessa made her mouth into an *O*.

"Wait a sec," I said.

"What?"

"If it's real, we're gonna want to scream, right?"

Tessa nodded. "*Oh*, yeah."

"But we can't," I said. "If the president's kids start screaming in the middle of the night..."

"Good point," Tessa said. "So how 'bout if we scream silently?"

"Pinky promise," I said. We hooked our fingers.

Tessa took a breath. "Here goes." She put one of the diamonds next to her face, made her lips into an *O* again and exhaled. I leaned close, and together we looked.

No fog.

No fog?

The diamond was real!

We closed our eyes, we opened our mouths, we pumped our fists—and we screamed!

Silently.

To somebody watching, it would've looked like the sound was on mute.

After that, Tessa and I took turns testing the other diamonds. And guess what? They were real, too. Every single one.

Hooligan must have been super tired because Tessa and I sneaked the collar back onto his neck without waking him. After that, the two of us were so excited there was no way we could go back to sleep.

So instead we brushed our teeth, washed our faces, got dressed, and made our beds. Ready to face the day, I looked at the clock on my bedside table.

It was four in the morning!

"Now what are we supposed to do?" I asked.

"Let's wake up Mom and Dad. This is big news!"

I shook my head. "We can't do that. Mom's tired already, and she has a country to run."

"Then let's look at your notes again," Tessa said. "Now that we know it couldn't have been ground up, we really have to find that diamond."

Instead of telling you every word Tessa and I said for the next three hours, I am going to summarize the important parts:

- Sometimes diamonds are cut more than once.
- Diamonds break compost grinders.
- Famous diamonds are priceless and worthless.

And

- The diamonds on Hooligan's collar test real.

This brought up three fat questions:

- Did the person/dog who sent the collar to Hooligan know it had real diamonds?
- If yes, why had he/she lied?
- And why was someone sending Hooligan diamonds at all?

At seven, Granny came in to wake us. You can imagine the look on her face when she saw us up and dressed. "What in the world...?"

"Well it *took* you long enough!" Tessa jumped off the sofa. "Come on. We have something to show you."

Shaking her head like we were crazy, Granny followed us into Hooligan's room. All three of us knelt down. All three of us looked in his crate.

All three of us saw it was empty!

CHAPTER FOURTEEN

"DOES what you want to show me have to do with Hooligan?" Granny asked.

"*Duh!*" Tessa said.

"Mr. Bryant took him out for a romp with Cottonball before Canine Class," Granny said.

"But that doesn't start for another hour!" Tessa said.

Granny shrugged. "He said there was no traffic this morning so he got here early. Come on and eat your breakfast. What's all the excitement anyway?"

It seemed lame just to tell Granny the diamonds were real. We wanted to prove it. Tessa said, "If it's okay, we'd rather tell you later."

"Suit yourselves," said Granny. "But remember you've got church this morning—right after Canine Class."

On our way to the kitchen, Tessa tried to argue: "We have to interview Mr. Mormora after class! It's really important!"

Granny's look said: Mr. Mormora can wait. God can't.

"Oh, *fine*," Tessa said.

"Meanwhile," Granny said brightly, "it's time to name the canary."

It was Nate's turn. And for once he had come to breakfast on time.

"I propose 'Serinus,'" he said.

"Se-whatziss?" Tessa asked.

"The Latin name for canary is *Serinus canaria domestica*," Nate said.

Granny cut bagels in half and put them in the toaster. "Sounds too much like sinus," she said, "and that gives me a headache."

Nate didn't seem too disappointed. "Did you know most male canaries sing all the time?"

"Maybe this guy would sing more if he had a name," Tessa said. "The last time he really sang out was on Friday—right before Hooligan went crazy."

"That reminds me of something," I said. "When Hooligan went crazy on Thursday? Remember how those birds outside were yakking? You could hear them over the helicopters."

Tessa nodded. "I do remember. Only what does that have to do with anything?"

Granny set down our toasted bagels and glasses of orange juice. We thanked her. I got out my notebook and wrote down about the singing canary and the yakking birds.

"I have no idea what it means," I told Tessa. "But it's another strange coincidence."

By the time Nate, Tessa and I got down to the South Lawn, Mr. Mormora was already there, and the puppies were starting to arrive. From beyond the fountain, Mr. Bryant, Cottonball and Hooligan were walking toward us.

Tessa and I still hadn't told anyone about the diamonds on the collar. And keeping it to herself was driving Tessa crazy. Finally she couldn't stand it. "Nathan, can you keep a secret? Hooligan's diamonds are real!"

Nate's mouth opened, like for a second he believed her. But then he started to argue: "They can't be.... The letter said...Who would send Hooligan real diamonds?"

Mr. Bryant by now was a few yards away. "Hello, girls. Hello, Nate." And a second later, Cottonball was threading his leash around Tessa's ankles while Hooligan, tail wagging, jumped up and tried to knock me over.

"*Sit*." I said.

Cottonball ignored me but Hooligan—future Top Dog—did as he was told.

"We can prove it, Nathan!" Tessa danced her ankles out of the tangle then bent down to undo Hooligan's collar.

Only there was one small problem.

The diamond collar was gone!

In its place was Hooligan's boring old brown collar—the one we had replaced when Empress Pu-Chi's gift arrived.

Tessa fell back on her bottom. My heart went thud. But before we could ask Mr. Bryant about it, Mr. Mormora called Canine Class to order.

CHAPTER FIFTEEN

THE Canine Class topic for the day was "stay."

And that—besides how Hooligan was perfect again—is pretty much all I remember. Otherwise, I was much too sleepy and much too distracted to pay attention.

Where was the diamond collar?

And something else was bugging me, too.

The collar had either disappeared in the night when Hooligan was in his crate or in the morning when Mr. Bryant was walking him. Could Mr. Bryant have taken it? Was it possible he knew the diamonds were real, too? Was it true he got to our house early because traffic was light—like he told Granny?

That wasn't a very good reason.

Mr. Bryant is Tessa's and my friend. But his daughter did need money....

I shook my head trying to get the thoughts inside to make sense. Something didn't seem right.

Anyway there was no time for questions. The moment

Canine Class was over, Dad herded Tessa and me toward the White House.

"But Dad!" Tessa protested. "Look!" She pointed at Hooligan's neck while we walked.

I thought we'd have to explain, but Dad understood right away. "That's strange. Where's the gift from the empress?"

Tessa got dramatic and waved her arms the way she does. "It's more than strange, Dad! Because it turns out the diamonds are *real!*"

Dad didn't argue like Nate did. He only raised his eyebrows. "When did you notice the collar was missing?"

Tessa took a breath. "Last night before bed I drank a glass of milk? And maybe my stomach was gurgly? Because in the night—"

Dad interrupted. "Short version."

"It was there about three thirty this morning," I said. "And gone at seven."

Dad's eyebrows stayed up. "Okay—you can explain in the car. You two go ahead and get dressed. Mom's in the Oval Office. I'm just going to touch base with her."

Mr. Ng met us outside the Dip Room.

"Good morning, Cameron. Good morning, Tessa. It's a beautiful day, don't you think?"

"Is it?" I hadn't even noticed, but he was right—blue sky and warm sun.

"Look, Mr. Ng! Hooligan's new collar is gone!" Tessa handed him Hooligan's leash. "And you know what else? The diamonds—"

"Tessa!" I said.

Tessa blinked. "What?"

But I couldn't tell her not to tell Mr. Ng right in front of Mr. Ng. It would be rude. "Nothing," I said. "Except we have to go. Come on."

"Have a good day, girls!" Mr. Ng called. And Hooligan woofed the same.

"Why did you make me be quiet?" Tessa said on the stairs. "Is Mr. Ng a suspect?"

"I don't know who's a suspect," I said. "But it can't be smart to tell everybody a bazillion dollars worth of diamonds are missing from the White House."

Tessa started to argue, but the words dissolved in a big, fat yawn. I think we were both grumpy from no sleep.

Like I said, the plan was for Mom to go to church with us, but a few minutes later when Tessa and I climbed into the car, we got another surprise. Only Dad and Malik were waiting.

Dad saw we were disappointed. "She's very sorry, girls. But something came up."

"Is it bad?" Tessa asked.

"I hope not," Dad said.

"What about Granny?" I said.

"She's going to another church today. A friend invited her."

Aunt Jen and Nate never go to church with us. They go to a different one that has mostly Korean people. That's because Nate was born in Korea, and Aunt Jen adopted him when he was a baby.

Our church is near Dupont Circle. So while we drove, Tessa told Dad the long version—how we tested the diamonds and sat up half the night. Dad didn't say much, but he listened carefully.

I complain about church sometimes, but really I like it. Instead of Sunday School, Tessa and I sit in the pew with our family. It's nice to be together. And anytime I get bored, there are the pretty windows to look at. Another part I like is hymns. Tessa sings loud, and I sing on key.

CHAPTER SIXTEEN

AT lunch, we got our first lucky break.

We didn't have to go looking everywhere for Mr. Mormora. He sat down to eat with us!

Only it seemed rude to interview a person who was eating a tuna melt. Wouldn't he get indigestion? So Tessa and I made a date to talk to him later.

Lunch was in the family dining room upstairs. The tuna melts came from the White House kitchen. They are Dad's favorite, and I like them, too, but they're messy. When I eat one the mayonnaise flies.

"So how do you think Hooligan is getting on in class?" Dad asked Mr. Mormora.

Mr. Mormora dabbed the corner of his mouth with his napkin. "Ah, you can see for yourself! He is an excellent student. He wants so much to make Cameron, his Canine Buddy, proud." He flashed me a smile, and I felt myself blush.

"There is, though, one thing that puzzles me," Mr. Mormora continued. "Hooligan is a little, uh...fleshier than I would like. And yet he is on an excellent diet with no opportunity for snacking. Can you explain that?" He looked at us each for an answer.

"Too many Canine Cookies?" said Tessa.

"No, no, no!" said Mr. Mormora. "Canine Cookies are specially formulated for good taste *and* good health."

I thought of Paul Song's dog. "Maybe someone's feeding him treats," I said.

Mr. Mormora nodded. "I have thought of this. It was the case with the dog I mentioned previously, Empress Pu-Chi. Her caregiver spoiled her with ginger snaps and liverwurst."

"*Ewww!*" said Tessa.

"What about this Mr. Ng?" said Mr. Mormora. "He is new, I believe. How well do you know him?"

Dad explained that anyone working in the White House has to be interviewed a bunch of times, then checked by the Secret Service.

"This tells us he is neither criminal nor spy," said Mr. Mormora. "But what is in his heart? Perhaps he is the kind that gives unhealthy treats to dogs to win their friendship."

And if that was true, I thought, could he also be the kind that stole diamond dog collars?

We finished our sandwiches and talked about the other dogs in Canine Class. As we were getting up, Mr. Mormora asked where we should meet.

"How about Mrs. Kennedy's Garden?" Tessa said. "There are chairs and a table out there."

"Perfect," said Mr. Mormora. "In half an hour?"

Back in our bedroom, Tessa and I changed out of

our church clothes. Then I got my notebook, and she put on her pink detecting hat. We were ready to go when Tessa asked me to bring the letter from Empress Pu-Chi. I found it in my top desk drawer and handed it over.

"But remember," I said, "Mr. Mormora is a witness, not a suspect. And we aren't gonna tell him the diamonds are real, right? It's a bad idea to blab that to everybody."

"Okay, okay. Don't give me a lecture," Tessa said. "Sheesh, you'd think I never interviewed a suspect before."

"*Witness*," I said.

"Right," Tessa said.

But I did not have a good feeling.

CHAPTER SEVENTEEN

UP till my aunt Jen, Jacqueline Kennedy was probably the prettiest First Lady ever. Her garden is outside the East Colonnade, which is the corridor that goes from the ground floor of the White House to the East Wing.

Malik came downstairs with Tessa and me, and he even offered to help us interview Mr. Mormora. "I'm a trained law enforcement professional, you know," he said.

"Thanks, Malik, but we've got this," Tessa said.

I looked at my sister. "We do?"

Tessa shrugged. "Sure. We have all the rest of March break to solve it, don't we? And not even any homework."

The Jacqueline Kennedy Garden has a lawn, hedges and flowerbeds. At one end is a pergola, sort of a stick house covered with vines. Mr. Mormora was waiting for us there. Granny said the vines would be leafy in the summer, but now they were just starting to show a little green.

Malik walked across the lawn and sat down in the shade on the other side. Tessa and I sat down on white metal chairs across from Mr. Mormora. Before I could even say hi, Tessa crossed her arms over her chest.

"Mr. Mormora," she said, "may I direct your attention to Exhibit A?"

I said, "Huh?"

Mr. Mormora said, "Huh?"

Tessa said, "*Duh!*" and waved the empress's letter in his face.

"May I see that please?" Mr. Mormora took the letter.

"Cammie and I know dogs can't write," Tessa said—like it proved we were unusually smart. "So do you know who wrote it for real?"

Mr. Mormora nodded. "I recognize the signature. It was written by the man who is responsible for the empress's personal correspondence. He is President Alfredo-Chin's chief of protocol, Mr. Eb Ghanamamma."

I was so surprised I stopped writing. "Eb Ghanamamma, the singer?"

Mr. Mormora smiled. "You have heard of him? It was very long ago that he gave up singing to become involved with politics."

"How come *I* never heard of him?" Tessa wanted to know.

"I was really little when Dad used to listen to him," I said. "He sang about people who were poor and a girl who was pretty."

Mr. Mormora nodded. "A folksinger, yes. His most famous song was a song of lost love called 'Lina.'"

"Did he ever sing about diamonds?" Tessa asked.

"Never," said Mr. Mormora.

Tessa looked disappointed. "So why would he want to send a zillion dollars worth to Hooligan then lie about it?"

If I was the kind of person who kicks her little sister, I would have kicked my little sister. "*Tessa!*" said.

"Oops," Tessa said.

But Mr. Mormora didn't look shocked . . . or guilty. "I do not know," he said. "And while I did not like Empress Pu-Chi, I found Mr. Ghanamamma very nice. I believe he sincerely wants to help the people. Perhaps you should ask him this question yourself? In fact . . ."

Mr. Mormora unhooked his phone from his belt then leaned over to show us the screen. He scrolled through pictures of dogs, tons of them, including the empress herself. She had a pouty face and a red bow tied between her ears. Then he scrolled through his contacts and found Eb Ghanamamma.

"Will this help you?" he asked.

Tessa said, "Write that down, Cammie," and jumped up from her chair. "We can phone right now! Thanks, Mr. Mormora."

"Aren't you forgetting something?" I said.

"Nope," said Tessa. "Let's go."

"The Canine Cookies?" I said. "That Hooligan found on the South Lawn?"

"Right!" Tessa recrossed her arms. "Mr. Mormora, if you were never out on the South Lawn before the first Canine Class, how come there were Canine Cookies everywhere for Hooligan to find? Did you lie to us on purpose, or what?"

Mr. Mormora looked confused.

I sighed. "You have to forgive my sister. She is very sleepy. What she's trying to say is Hooligan found a whole bunch of Canine Cookies on the South Lawn yesterday. Do you have any idea how they got there?"

"Now that I find interesting," said Mr. Mormora. "I did not drop the cookies, if that is what you mean. But we have been keeping the cookie supply in one of the outdoor sheds. Yesterday before class, a box disappeared. I thought I had miscounted, but perhaps...?" He shrugged.

I scribbled this down and stood up. "Come on, Tessa. Now we can call. Thanks, Mr. Mormora!"

He had been a big help—that is, if he was telling the truth. But if he was a diamond thief, wouldn't he have lied to throw us off the track?

CHAPTER EIGHTEEN

OTHER than Nate, Tessa and I are the only kids in America who don't have cell phones. Because of that, we would have to call Mr. Ghanamamma from a White House phone. Malik came upstairs with us, but he didn't have to stick around once we were safe on the second floor. Since we needed privacy, we decided to use the phone on the desk in the Treaty Room.

On our way, I thought of something. "What time is it in a certain nearby nation?"

Tessa consulted Barbie. "Four o'clock."

"It might be a different time zone there," I said. "We might call Mr. Ghanamamma and wake him in the middle of the night."

"Well, *that* would be embarrassing," said Tessa.

Since Nate has a computer in his bedroom, we went upstairs to ask him. "I'll go online and check," he said. And the way it turned out, Tessa was right—four o'clock in the nearby nation, too.

"But why do you need to know?" Nate asked.

Explaining took a while.

"So you're really going to call him?" Nate said. "You don't think you'll get in trouble?"

Tessa and I looked at each other. Mom had told us not to phone presidents. But she never said not to phone a chief of protocol. Right?

"We're detecting," Tessa said finally. "Someone has to do it."

"Can I come?" said Nate.

Tessa and I looked at each other. We didn't necessarily get along all the time with Nate. But Tessa shrugged okay, so I said, "I guess. It could be helpful, having someone who knows everything."

The Treaty Room is at the top of the grand stairway and next to the Lincoln Bedroom on the second floor. Sometimes Mom works there, but today she was working in the Oval Office. It's in the West Wing, which is supposedly part of the White House but really more like a separate building next door.

We took the elevator down from the third floor. When we walked out, we saw that Hooligan was in his old bed by the fireplace in the West Sitting Hall, and Mr. Ng was sitting on the comfy sofa, reading the newspaper. I had a sudden idea.

"Can we borrow Hooligan? We need a guard dog."

Mr. Ng thought for a moment. "It *should* be fine," he finally said. "I believe he is too tired to get himself in any trouble."

In the Treaty Room, I closed the door and ordered Hooligan to sit and stay.

"Your job is to guard the door," I told him. "If you hear anybody coming, bark!"

Hooligan smiled an agreeable doggy smile. Then he lay down and closed his eyes. A minute later, he was chasing rabbits in his sleep. Some guard dog.

Next, we decided Tessa would do the talking. I didn't want to say it, but I was worried about having to speak a foreign language. In school, my worst subject is spelling but my second worst is Spanish. And anyway, none of us was totally sure what language they spoke in the nearby nation.

Tessa said it didn't matter. "I'll just talk loud. Ready, Nate?"

He dialed. It was a lot of numbers. But somebody must have picked up fast because Tessa tilted her head to listen. Then she smiled and said, "WHATEVER YOU SAID, BACK AT YOU. I AM TESSA PARKS FROM THE UNITED STATES OF AMERICA. CAN I TALK TO EB GHANAMAMMA?"

There was a pause. "WARM AND SUNNY, THANK YOU. IS THE WEATHER NICE IN YOUR NATION?" Another pause. "YES. EB GHANAMAMMA. DON'T ASK ME TO SPELL IT. I CAN HARDLY SAY IT."

After a moment, she spoke to Nate and me. "I'm on hold."

"I don't get it," Nate said, "did they speak English?"

Tessa shook her head. "Of course not—*duh*. It's a foreign country."

"Then what was that stuff about the weather?"

Tessa shrugged. "Grown-ups always talk about

the weather." She tilted her head again. "MR. GHANA-MAMMA?" Pause. "WELL, *THAT'S* DISAPPOINTING. WHERE?" Pause. Then she repeated her name, gave the White House phone number, said GOOD-BYE and hung up.

"What happened?" Nate and I asked at the same time.

"HE'S IN THE JUNGLE," Tessa said.

"STOP SHOUTING!" I said.

"What jungle?" Nate said

"Whatever jungle's in a certain nearby nation. Anyway, there's no cell service there. So he can't be reached."

"Wait a sec," said Nate. "How did you know the word for jungle in a foreign language?"

Tessa thought for a second. "I don't know. I just did. Or maybe it was *beach*. Anyway, he definitely wasn't there and could not be reached."

"So when will he be back?" I asked.

"Earth to Cammie?" said Tessa. "How do I know? They weren't speaking English!"

CHAPTER NINETEEN

HOOLIGAN had slept through Tessa's shouting, but now came a noise so shrill and piercing he sprang up like a jack-in-the-box: *aw-row-row-row-row-rowff!*

"What is it, puppy?" Tessa ran and opened the door to the hall to look. Standing on the other side was Ms. Kootoor, but she hadn't made the noise. She was as startled as we were.

Hooligan is always glad to see Ms. Kootoor and shot out the door. But this time he didn't knock her over. She was ready.

Meanwhile, the nameless canary sang—*Twee-twee-twee!*—Granny and Mr. Bryant appeared in the doorway on our left, and a second later Cottonball careened between them and leaped toward Hooligan, who forgot all about Ms. Kootoor and wrestled his puppy pal to the rug.

For a few seconds the two of them played, then Hooligan broke free and sprinted toward the East Hall with Cottonball close behind. Now the second floor was a race track, with Hooligan and Cottonball neck and neck. Every once in a while a tail hit a wall, the furniture, or some fragile historic object.

Here is a piece of advice if you ever live with a dog: Don't put breakable things at tail level.

Mr. Bryant and Mr. Ng moved to the Center Hall to stop them, but it wasn't easy. There was lots of furniture in the way, and the dogs could go under and around places Mr. Bryant and Mr. Ng couldn't. Just watching made me dizzy, and then Mr. Bryant wasn't looking and collided with Mr. Ng, and they both fell back and sat down on the rug—*ouch*.

"Everyone just stay calm!" Granny said, not very calmly. "If we wait, they'll tire themselves out." But then, "*Oh!*" she had to sidestep to stay out of Cottonball's way, and "*Ooh!*" Hooligan brushed by on the other side.

It was Mr. Mormora who saved the day. The stairs outside his room come out on the second floor near the Treaty Room. When he heard the commotion, he came running down and placed himself in the dogs' path like a traffic cop. "Gentlemen?" he said. "You stop now."

And they did.

It took three maids to sweep and dust and set things right. Meanwhile, Mr. Ng took the dogs outside, Ms. Kootoor said she had a headache and went back to her room and Mr. Mormora went back upstairs. In the end, it was Granny, Mr. Bryant, Tessa, Nate and I who collapsed in the West Sitting Hall.

Maybe for the first time ever, Granny looked

embarrassed. "I guess I shouldn't have tested it with the dogs around," she said. "It seems to have upset them."

"Tested what?" Tessa asked.

From her pocket, Granny pulled two silver some-things, each one on a chain—whistles! "I thought Ms. Kootoor's father's idea was a good one," she went on. "So these are for you girls."

"Cool!" Tessa took a whistle and immediately put it to her mouth.

"*No!*" everybody shouted at once.

Tessa grinned. "Only kidding. Thanks, Granny. Even if it doesn't have diamonds, I like it better than Ms. Kootoor's. It's a lot bigger."

I took my whistle and thanked Granny, too. Then I realized this might be our best chance to interview Mr. Bryant. Tessa must've been thinking the same thing because she crossed her arms over her chest. "Mr. Bryant," she said. "Do you mind if we ask you a few questions?"

CHAPTER TWENTY

"QUESTIONS?" said Mr. Bryant. "No, I don't mind. Are you girls detecting again? I understand those diamonds on Hooligan's collar might be real after all."

"How'd you hear that?" Tessa asked.

Granny looked embarrassed again. Twice in one afternoon had to be some kind of record. "I think by now it's, uh...general knowledge here in the White House," she said.

Tessa started over. "Mr. Bryant, was Hooligan wearing his diamond collar when you got him out of his crate this morning?"

Mr. Bryant shook his head. "No. In fact, he wasn't wearing any collar at all. That's why I put the old one back on him."

"What time did that happen?" Tessa asked.

"Must've been just after six twenty," Mr. Bryant said. "I know because they clocked me in at the gatehouse at six fifteen."

"So that means the collar disappeared between—" I

started to say. But I was interrupted by the appearance of two men in almost identical gray suits standing in the doorway to the center hall. Granny seemed to know them.

"Yes?" she said.

"Sorry to bother you, ma'am," said the taller one. "Do you mind if we—?"

"No, no. Go ahead," Granny said. "Whatever you need."

"Thank you," said the other man, and they turned and disappeared back into the hall.

Some parts of the White House are public spaces, but the second and third floors are where we live. That means I usually know everyone. But I didn't know these guys.

"What's going on?" I asked.

"Are they gonna look in our room?" Tessa asked.

"They're doing their job," Granny said, which, if you think about it, did not answer the question. "Your mom will be in to talk to you later."

"Oh, *fine*," said Tessa. "As usual, the grown-ups are all in on it together."

CHAPTER TWENTY-ONE

NO way was Granny giving us more information. So Tessa and I went back to our room to look at our latest notes. Unfortunately, it seemed like they only added confusion.

Then I remembered something Granny once told Tessa and me—how a fresh pair of eyes can help you see clearly.

Could Nate's be a fresh pair of eyes?

Tessa didn't like the idea at first, but in the end I talked her into it. "Only we have to make him pinky promise not to reveal our secrets," she said.

"*Ewww!*" said Nate, when we proposed the pinky promise, but in the end, curiosity won out, and we all hooked fingers.

"Don't you ever tell any of my friends I did this *ever*," he said when we let go.

"The problem," I said after he had looked at my notebook, "is that the investigation keeps changing. At first we were only looking for a single fake diamond.

Now we're looking for a single real diamond, plus the collar."

"But that's a good thing," said Nate. "It's like a math problem. Adding a second variable limits the possible solutions."

Tessa shook her head. "Would you puh-leeze remember I am only in second grade?"

"Even you can understand this, Tessa," Nate said. "The way you've got it figured, the diamond disappeared when Hooligan was in the trees by the tennis courts, right? Then the collar disappeared between four and six twenty this morning. So if you forget all the confusing details about Mr. Ghanamamma and El Brillante, the thief has to be someone who could've gotten to Hooligan *both* times. That's fewer people than had access to him one time or the other. See?"

"But couldn't there be two different thieves?" I said. "Like, Mr. Mormora doesn't seem to trust Mr. Ng. He thinks Mr. Ng's giving Hooligan treats that make him fat."

"Yeah—and then there's these new guys," Tessa said, "the ones in the suits? Who are they anyway? There were all kinds of people on the lawn Thursday. Maybe they were there, too."

"I don't know who they are," said Nate. "But it seems illogical for there to be two thieves—too big a coincidence."

I was trying to be logical, but I didn't like where logic was going. To me, it seemed obvious that the person with the best opportunity to steal first the diamond and then the collar was—

"Mr. Bryant," Tessa said my thought out loud. "He fits Nate's math problem. He was around Hooligan and the collar both times. But that doesn't matter because we know Mr. Bryant didn't do it."

"How do we know?" Nate said.

"Because he's Mr. Bryant!" Tessa said.

"I have an idea," said Nate. "The first diamond disappeared during the helicopter chase, right? Maybe we can review the videos."

"Hey!" I said. "I know someone who can help. I can ask her tomorrow at Canine Class."

At bedtime, Mom had barely opened our door when Tessa pounced. "Who are those guys in the gray suits, anyway?"

Mom frowned. "I missed you, too, Muffin."

Tessa said, "Sorry, Mama. I love you. Who are those guys in the gray suits?"

Mom sighed and sat down on the edge of my bed. "I need to tell you both something, but I don't want you to worry. Canine Class is going to go on tomorrow as usual, but starting tonight, the White House is on heightened security alert. The two men are part of my national security team."

Tessa looked at me. "Translation?"

"She means they're part of the government, and they're being extra careful because bad guys might try to do something. Right?"

"More or less," Mom said.

Tessa squealed. *"Bad guys?!"*

"Shhh!" Mom put her fingers to Tessa's lips. "It's only a precaution. For a few days, the Secret Service will have a little extra help here in the White House. And you girls and your cousin will have to stick around, too. But there's a silver lining. Dad had been planning to work in California this week, and now he's going to stay here with us."

Sometimes when you're thinking hard about something, it seems like everything's connected. "Mom—does the security alert have anything to do with what Tessa and I are investigating?"

Mom's expression didn't change, but she stood up. "What you and Tessa are investigating?" she said. "Well, I should say."

I looked over at Tessa. "Was that a yes?"

"No idea," said Tessa. "Mom, was that a—" but the question turned into a giggle because Mom was tickling her. "*Mama-a-a-a!*" She was still giggling. "Sto-o-op!"

Mom's tickling became a snuggle and a kiss. Then it was my turn, and then—before we could ask more questions—Mom was heading out the door. "Good night, muffins," she said. "I love you."

CHAPTER TWENTY-TWO

WAS Mr. Bryant a thief?

Or Mr. Ng?

And what about the guys in the gray suits?

Was Mom investigating the missing diamonds?

And who was giving Hooligan fattening treats?

All those questions were on my mind when I woke up. But in the kitchen, Granny reminded me about something *way* more important—my turn to name the canary.

"How about Singalong?" I tried.

Before Granny could even express an opinion, Tessa was shaking her head. "No way! That's the same as Paul Song's dog. It would be confusing!"

"Confusing, how? It's not like the canary will ever even meet Paul Song's dog."

"And besides—" Tessa totally ignored my excellent point—"you stole that idea, Cammie. I think the nameless canary needs an original name, one that's all his own."

Granny sighed. "It should be a name we can agree on at least. Your turn tomorrow, Tessa."

The Canine Class topic of the day was "heel," and Hooligan got it right away. I didn't want to jinx it by talking about it, but at this rate he for sure was going to be Top Dog.

With the security alert, all the CBs and CITs had to be double-checked when they entered the White House grounds. Because of that, there was no time before class to arrange help with the videos. It was only when Mr. Mormora practiced with the other dogs that I got my chance.

Ms. Major and her cockapoo, Pickles, were next to me as usual. Pickles was trying to untie Ms. Major's shoelaces with his teeth. "Ms. Major," I said, "did I get it right that you keep track of news stories about us and Hooligan?"

Ms. Major tried to bump Pickles away without actually kicking him. It looked like she was tap dancing. "Indeed I do," she said.

"Then can I ask a favor? Is there a chance my sister, my cousin and I could look at some TV stories from Thursday afternoon?"

"Sure—there are plenty, and I'd be happy to help." Ms. Major stopped dancing to check the calendar on her phone. Pickles went back to chewing her laces. "How about one o'clock—right after lunch?"

"We'll be there," I said. "Thanks."

* * *

Ms. Major's office is in the West Wing. My mom's office, the Oval Office, is there, too. Mom's is really nice, but a lot of the West Wing is so crowded it's crazy. Almost everyone works in a cubicle, which is a room with no door and thin pretend walls.

Malik was on duty again, so Tessa, Nate and I had come downstairs with him. Trying to find Ms. Major was like being trapped in a maze. Finally, Malik called out: "Hello-o-o? Ms. Ann Major, are you there?"

When an answering voice called, "Hello-o-o-o!," we followed it and found her.

"Welcome to my world," Ms. Major said. It was a tiny space with bare walls except for a calendar turned to last January. The picture on it was a German shepherd. There was no place for four people to sit down, so we crowded around her desk. On it were an old, boxy computer, binders, papers and photos of Pickles.

"As you know, several stations covered the events on Thursday," she said. "So I pulled up four examples— Fox, CNN, CBS and the local news with Jan and Larry. We could probably find more if you need them."

It took us about half an hour to watch the four clips. A lot was the same, of course, but there were differences. Like three of the announcers treated the story mostly like a joke, and one treated it like the whole country had spun out of control. Also there were different views, depending on where the camera guys were standing.

The longest report was Jan and Larry's.

It started with a close-up of Hooligan before he

broke his leash, and Jan's voice saying, "With his diamond dog collar, the presidential pooch sported a glamorous new look this afternoon. But soon thereafter, chaos erupted on the South Lawn!"

"Ms. Major," Nate interrupted. "Could you go back over that part, please?"

"Sure." She restarted it.

"Look at that," Nate said. "When Hooligan turns, you can see all the diamonds—twelve of 'em."

What happened next on the video wasn't a picture, it was noise—the yakking birds. After that, Hooligan took off running with Tessa after him, her hair blowing everywhere, her eyes tearing in the wind.

"Well, *that's* not very flattering," she said.

The clip went on to show the parade of pursuers— with a close-up of the vice president—and even a view of flowers being crushed by stomping feet. Jan and Larry took turns narrating. At one point Jan said, "Look at that, Larry. For a time, when he was near the tennis courts, Hooligan eluded his pursuers altogether!"

"Bingo," said Nate.

"Is that what you were after?" Ms. Major asked.

"Partly," said Nate, "but keep going."

Now the view pulled back to a bunch of confused-looking people searching for Hooligan by the bushes near the garden plot. Among them were Tessa and the vice president, but you couldn't see Mr. Bryant. Maybe he was there, but he wasn't in the shot.

The final few seconds showed Dad's helicopter

landing and then Ms. Kootoor—cameraman catnip—with Hooligan licking her face.

"I guess all's well that ends well," said the voice of Larry.

"Bow wow to that," said Jan. "In other news..."

Ms. Major stopped the video on the last frame. Nate pointed to the screen. "See that?" It was another view of Hooligan's collar, and guess what? A diamond was missing.

Ms. Major looked at her watch. Like everyone who works for my mom, she must've been super busy. "Did you get what you need?"

"I think so," I said. "It was really nice of you to help us. Thanks."

"No problem," she said. "Would you like me to e-mail you the links? Then you can watch the stories on your own if you want to."

"E-mail them to me," Nate said. "I'm the only one with a computer in my room."

Tessa said, "Must be *nice*," and stuck out her tongue when he wasn't looking.

Nobody talked as we left the West Wing. Malik was concentrating on finding a route out of the maze. Nate, Tessa and I were putting together what the video had told us. We now knew for sure that Hooligan himself had disappeared for a few minutes. And so had Mr. Bryant. Did the diamond just fall off the collar? Or did somebody take it?

Tessa said we should flat out ask Mr. Bryant.

Nate said that was crazy. "If he took it, he'll lie and say he didn't. If he didn't, he'll be mad we accused him."

"He might confess," Tessa said.

"Lame," Nate said.

"Maybe we need a break," I said.

Nate said fine. He was going to find Jeremy and shoot some hoops.

Tessa said, "I know—how 'bout if we dress Hooligan up in outfits and take pictures?"

This was not my first-choice idea. But I knew if I said no, she'd want to play Barbies—and that's worse.

We found Mr. Bryant and Hooligan in the West Sitting Hall.

"Be my guest," Mr. Bryant told us. "But you must promise to keep him under control. I'll just get myself a cup of coffee and check back."

Hooligan absolutely refused to step into Tessa's flamingo rain boots. But he didn't seem to mind the pink kimono, or the plastic pearls.

"Pretty puppy!" said Tessa, clicking the camera in his face.

"He's totally embarrassed," I said.

"He likes it!" Tessa said. "Hey, we can send these pictures to the Empress Pu-Chi! She of all dogs would appreciate them."

"We can put them in with the thank-you note," I said.

Tessa shook her head. "I'm pretty sure—and Aunt Jen will back me up—that when the gift's been stolen, you don't have to write a thank-you note."

"Really? High five!" I guess it's true there's always a bright side.

CHAPTER TWENTY-THREE

MOM had to eat dinner with her advisers in the Oval Office. At bedtime, Dad came in to give us our kisses. Nothing against Dad, but I was really missing my mom.

The next morning, I woke up even before Granny came in. So did Tessa. "I've got a really good name for the canary," she announced.

Oh, fine. My mom's gone AWOL. Bad guys are threatening. Diamonds are missing. And my sister's all happy because she's got a name for the canary! Was this supposed to brighten my day?

When we got to the kitchen, Nate was already there. And so was Ms. Kootoor. I guess one thing about getting up early is you get used to getting up early.

"This is your moment, Tessa," I said. "What's the 'really good' name?"

"Ghanamamma!" she cried.

I had been expecting to hate it, but instead I cracked up—Nate, too. Then we heard a thump. Ms. Kootoor had been standing by the breakfast table. When I turned, I saw she had dropped her Blueberry Bag—*thump*—to the floor. Her face looked whiter than usual, too.

"Are you okay?" Granny asked.

Ms. Kootoor smiled weakly. "Got out of bed too fast, I guess. Uh...what was that name, Tessa?"

"Ghanamamma. It's the name of somebody—" Tessa didn't finish her sentence. I guess she suddenly remembered how we weren't going to advertise that we'd phoned a certain nearby nation.

"Somebody?" Ms. Kootoor prompted.

"A singer my dad used to like," said Tessa.

Before Ms. Kootoor could ask for details, Mr. Bryant came in with Hooligan.

"How's everyone this morning?" he asked, then he turned to the canary. "Have these kids come up with a name for you yet?"

"How do you know we're naming the canary?" Tessa asked.

"It was my idea," said Mr. Bryant.

Tessa looked at Granny. "Is that true?"

Granny gave Mr. Bryant a look. I don't know what there was about it, but all of a sudden I got a funny feeling.

"Yes, it's true," Granny said. "And they haven't named him yet. Some of their ideas are real humdingers, though."

Mr. Bryant stroked his chin. "Hmm. What's the matter with that name for a canary? Humdinger?"

"I like it!" said Tessa.

"Cammie? Nate?" Granny asked.

"I'm down," I said.

Nate sighed. "If you all prefer Humdinger to Serinus..."

"Then it's settled," said Granny. And what she did next almost knocked me over. She kissed Mr. Bryant on the cheek!

"I think I'm still in shock," said Nate a few minutes later. Along with Hooligan, we were heading to the South Lawn for Canine Class.

Mr. Bryant had gone down already to get Cottonball. Ms. Kootoor had gone back to her room to lie down.

I shook my head. "So the way it turns out, Mr. Bryant gave her the canary."

"And that date Mr. Bryant went out on...?" Tessa said.

"And when Granny went to church with 'a friend'...?" I said.

"Not to mention the tennis date," Tessa said.

"And all the coffee they've both been drinking!" Nate said.

Talking about it, we walked slower and slower. Now, in the hall outside the Dip Room, we stopped altogether. "I'm not sure how I feel about Granny dating Mr. Bryant," Tessa said. "But there is one good thing. For sure Mr. Bryant has to be innocent. Granny would never date a diamond thief."

Canine Class that day was review—sit, stay and heel. I remembered how Mr. Mormora had predicted that by graduation all the dogs would be "models of canine class." Mostly he was right. Pickles still got distracted, and the Chihuahua forever wanted his belly scratched. But most of the dogs were getting the hang of good behavior.

And Hooligan was on track to be Top Dog!

When class was almost over, Mr. Mormora made an announcement: "Tomorrow is our graduation ceremony. We have planned some surprises, so please be sure your canines look their best. Also, if any of you wishes to say good-bye to me, may I ask you to stay after class today? Because after class tomorrow, I have a plane to catch. I have been asked by an old friend to go with him on safari!"

CHAPTER TWENTY-FOUR

YOU might have noticed, if you're paying attention, that for all the detecting Tessa, I and Nate had done, we still had not

- found the first diamond
- found the other 11 diamonds
- figured out who stole them
- figured out if their disappearance was connected to El Brillante, the missing diamond in a certain nearby nation.

In fact, the only mystery we'd solved was one we weren't trying to solve: where Granny's canary came from.

As detectives we were totally lame.

After lunch, Tessa, Nate, Jeremy and I went outside to play Frisbee with Hooligan on the lawn. This lasted about fifteen minutes. The wind had picked up after Canine Class, and by now it was gray and freezing outside!

I've lived in Washington ever since Mom first was

elected to the Senate. For Tessa, that's her whole life. But Nate just moved from San Diego in January. He was shivering. "I thought winter was over!" he said.

"March is always like this," I told him. "Sometimes it even snows."

"What if we go bowling?" Nate asked. The White House has a bowling alley on the ground floor. We had only been there a couple of times. Usually we were too busy.

"Bad news on bowling," said Jeremy. "I understand they're refinishing the lane. It should be dry by the end of the week, though."

In the end, we were so desperate we decided to watch TV in the Solarium. Of course, the second we got there, Nate grabbed the remote. And what did he turn on? News!

Tessa said, "*Ewwww!*," and I tackled him, but he held the remote away so I couldn't get it, then Tessa jumped and almost had it, but he said, "Hey, wait—look!" which I thought was a trick, but it turned out not to be. The picture on the screen was a dog with a red bow in her hair, the Empress Pu-Chi!

I don't mean the actual empress. I mean a photo of her on a sign outside a palace in the capital city of the nearby nation. There was writing in a foreign language on the sign, too. The news guy translated: "People are more important than dogs!"

According to the news guys, protesters in the nearby nation believed Empress Pu-Chi was treated better than poor people, and they wanted a new government.

"You mean they want to fire President Alfredo-Chin?" said Tessa. "But I like him! He forgave Hooligan, and Mom says he's a friend of the American people."

"Mr. Mormora doesn't like him," I remembered. "Do you think Mr. Mormora is on the side of the protesters?"

The news guy was still talking. "Opposition forces say their major stumbling block is raising the financial means necessary to effect change...."

"What is he talking about now?" Tessa looked at Nate.

"The people who want a different government need money to get one," Nate said.

"Is Mr. Ghanamamma one of those people?" asked Tessa.

Nate shook his head no. "He works for President Alfredo-Chin."

"But Mr. Mormora said he used to sing about poor people and beautiful women," said Tessa. "That makes him sound like more of a protester."

"And now he's gone to the jungle," I said.

Then I thought of something—don't safaris happen in jungles?

"You guys?" I said. "I just thought of something...."

"So did I," said Nate. "The protesters need money to change the government, right? Well, one way to get money is to work for it. But another is...."

"Steal it," said Tessa.

"Or steal something valuable—like a diamond," said Nate.

Sometimes thoughts are like rolling snowballs—they

grow and grow, out of control. All of a sudden we couldn't think—or talk—fast enough. "You mean El Brillante," I said. "But it's famous like the Hope Diamond, worth everything and nothing."

"Do you have your notebook, Cammie?" Tessa asked. "I want to see something."

The television was still talking, but we had stopped watching. We were huddled together on the floor, reading over pages of notes.

"There!" Tessa pointed. "That's what I remembered. Mr. Rubio said sometimes diamonds are cut up into smaller diamonds. So if you needed to get money from a famous diamond, couldn't you cut it up? And sell the pieces?"

Nate was nodding. "If that's true, it could be there's not just a connection between Hooligan's diamonds and El Brillante—Hooligan's diamonds *are* El Brillante."

Now it was like our snowball had become an avalanche. "Are you saying the protesters stole the diamond, cut it up, put the pieces on a collar and mailed it to Hooligan?" I asked.

"Bingo," said Tessa.

"But there's a million problems with that!" I said. "I mean, how do you get money from Hooligan? And besides, the collar came from the Empress Pu-Chi—with a letter from Mr. Ghanamamma. Like Nate just said, he's not a protester."

Nate the know-it-all rolled his eyes like I was the dumbest cousin ever. "Pay attention, Cameron. Let's say Tessa's got it right about Mr. Ghanamamma. Let's say he's secretly on the side of the protesters. When he sent the collar here, he wasn't really sending it to Hooligan. He was sending it to a confederate."

"What's confederate?" said Tessa.

"Someone he knew he could trust," said Nate, "someone who would sell the diamonds then send back the money."

Tessa was nodding. "But before that person could sell the diamonds," she said, "they would have to steal the diamonds. So if we find the confederate, then we've found the thief."

CHAPTER TWENTY-FIVE

NATE and Tessa's theories were giving me a headache.

But I had to admit they made a weird kind of sense. And my own puzzle piece fit, too. "Guys?" I said. "There's something else. Mr. Ghanamamma's in the jungle, right? And Mr. Mormora says he's going on safari? So that might mean—"

"Mr. Mormora is going to meet up with Mr. Ghanamamma!" Tessa finished my sentence. "He's the confederate. He's the thief."

"Too easy," said Nate. "If Mr. Mormora was the confederate, he wouldn't have told us he knew Empress Pu-Chi and spent time in the nearby nation. He would have tried to keep all that a secret."

"Maybe he thought we'd find out anyway," I said.

Nate shook his head. "I'm betting it's Mr. Bryant."

"But Granny—" Tessa began.

"That's part of his plot, Tessa," Nate said. "He's

pretending to like Granny, just like Mr. Ghanamamma pretended he was working for President Alfredo-Chin. If Mr. Bryant's the thief, he probably thinks his friendship with Granny will protect him. Except for you guys, he's the one who's closest to Hooligan. If the protesters in the nearby nation wanted to recruit someone to help them, that's who they'd go to."

"But Mr. Bryant doesn't care about a nearby nation," Tessa said. "Does he?"

"I bet they're paying him a bundle of money," Nate said.

"Unless it's Mr. Ng," I said.

Tessa and Nate looked at me.

"Where did that come from?" Nate asked.

"Mr. Bryant's worked in the White House forever," I said, "but Mr. Ng came to work right before the collar arrived and right after El Brillante was stolen. That was—" I looked at my notes—"sometime in the last month, according to Jan and Larry."

Nate and Tessa were listening like this made sense. But the truth is I was making it up as I went along. I just didn't want the thief to be Mr. Bryant.

"Uh...," I said, "and...well, Mr. Mormora thinks Mr. Ng is feeding Hooligan unhealthy treats. So maybe he is, and he's doing it, uh...so Hooligan will be his special friend and come whenever he calls. Like maybe on Thursday, he called Hooligan when he was down in the trees by the tennis court hiding."

Tessa nodded. "Good thinking, Cammie."

"You're kidding," I said.

"No, seriously," said Tessa. "I am officially completely confused. If you ask me, they all did it. But there's still something I can't figure out. Where are the diamonds now?"

CHAPTER TWENTY-SIX

IN Nate's room we looked up El Brillante on the computer and learned it weighed sixty karats. Divided by twelve, it would break up into new diamonds that were about five karats each. When we found a picture of a five karat diamond, it looked like the ones on the collar. In other words, it was big and fat for a diamond but small for anything else, about the size of a jelly bean.

Finding twelve jelly beans in the White House would be impossible! In case you don't know, the White House is huge—132 rooms in the main part, plus work rooms and storage areas—not to mention the grounds outside.

Besides, the diamonds might already be gone.

Or maybe not? With the security alert, people going in and out were being checked super carefully—even the staff. It could be that whoever had the diamonds was waiting till it was safer to take them away.

"I have one last idea," said Tessa dramatically. "And if it doesn't work, I am officially giving up."

On our way down to the second floor, we ran into Mr. Bryant and Hooligan in the elevator. It was a little strange seeing Mr. Bryant. We not only thought he might be a diamond thief; we also thought he might be lying to our very own Granny about how much he liked her.

And then he said, "Just the people I was looking for! Would you kids mind watching the star pupil for a while? I thought I might get a cup of coffee."

"With Granny?" Tessa asked suspiciously.

"Why, yes, as a matter of fact," said Mr. Bryant. "Uh...do you have a problem with that?"

Tessa sighed and looked at me, then Nate. "I guess not," she said. "Come on, puppy."

Tessa's idea was to interview Mrs. Hedges. We found her coming out of the Lincoln Bedroom. She had a vacuum cleaner in one hand and a rag in the other. Of course, Hooligan was delighted to see his old pal, and lunged—causing Mrs. Hedges to drop everything and duck behind a sofa.

"Hooligan, *heel!*" I said.

Hooligan stopped and looked back, like, Do I have to? But then he circled around and dropped to his haunches beside me the way he'd been taught. "Good dog!"

Now Mrs. Hedges peeked over the sofa and narrowed her eyes. "That dog doesn't fool me. As soon as these classes are over, he'll be back to his old tricks."

"Mrs. Hedges," Tessa crossed her arms over her chest. "We have a few questions for you."

Keeping an eye on Hooligan, Mrs. Hedges came

around to our side of the sofa, sat and made herself comfortable. "Go ahead. I don't mind getting off my feet. That woman Ms. Kootoor is more trouble than half a dozen normal—"

"Mrs. Hedges—" Tessa tried to interrupt.

"—it took a whiskbroom, the vacuum cleaner, and furniture oil to get the dried mud off her closet floor. And there's that cooler she keeps. The ice needs replacing twice a day! What's she need a cooler for? The White House food isn't good enough? Anyway, I've only got one more day of putting up with her. She's packing to leave tomorrow. Now that Mr. Mormora, on the other hand, I'll be sorry—"

"Mrs. Hedges?" Tessa tried again.

"Yes?" Mrs. Hedges said.

"While you've been cleaning and stuff, have you noticed twelve mysterious diamonds lying around?"

"Subtle," Nate said.

Mrs. Hedges looked shocked. "Now, you children know I can't go talking about what I see. There is such a thing as privacy."

"We know," I said quickly. "And we would never even ask. Only it's really important."

"To the future of a nearby nation," Nate said.

"Not to mention Granny's happiness," I said.

"And Hooligan's," Tessa said.

"All that?" said Mrs. Hedges. "Well, let me think." Approximately two seconds passed, then, "Nope." She shrugged. "No diamonds. Sorry."

* * *

True to her word, Tessa gave up.

And after I had finished writing down my notes, I did, too.

At dinnertime, Dad and Granny ate with us, but Aunt Jen and Mom were too busy. Later, we watched a movie called *That Darn Cat* in the White House theater. It was Mr. Mormora's suggestion. It turns out he doesn't even have a dog of his own. In his off hours, he prefers cats.

Dad came in to kiss us good night.

"*Again?*" Tessa said. "We haven't seen Mom all day."

"If it's any consolation, I've barely seen her myself," Dad said. "And that brings me to some news. Good or bad first?"

"Bad!" I said.

"Good!" Tessa said.

Dad had a quarter in his pocket. When he flipped it, Tessa called tails and won. "The crisis your mom's been working on? It should blow over tomorrow. And then she'll have some time. If it warms back up, maybe a picnic."

Tessa pumped her fist—"*Yes!*"—but I was too worried about the bad news.

"And?" I said.

"Well . . . okay. The thing is, I don't want to upset you. . . ."

"Uh oh," said Tessa.

"But perhaps you've heard there's some trouble in a certain nearby nation—"

"Protesters!" Tessa interrupted.

Dad nodded. "And quite unexpectedly those troubles have spilled over into the United States. In fact, tomorrow morning after Canine Class, there's going to be an arrest made here at the White House. The timing is unfortunate, but necessary. I'm telling you because I don't want you to be alarmed. At the same time, just in case there's an emergency, it's important that you stay out of the way."

Of course we had a million questions. Like who was going to be arrested? And what had they done? And was it because of the diamond dog collar?

But Dad just shook his head. "I can't say anymore, I'm sorry." After that, he gave us our kisses and said, "Sweet dreams."

After the door closed, the dark in our room seemed especially dark. Then Tessa asked, "Did Dad say emergency?"

"He said *maybe* emergency."

"Same difference," said Tessa. "So I know just what we need to take to Canine Class—our emergency whistles! That's why Granny gave them to us, right?"

CHAPTER TWENTY-SEVEN

SWEET dreams?

Ha!

Falling asleep was worse than on Christmas Eve, and instead of presents, my dreams were full of handcuffs and escaping canines, not to mention diamonds, diamonds everywhere.

It felt like I hadn't slept at all when someone shook my shoulder. Granny never does that. "Wha—hello, who?" I opened my eyes, and I couldn't believe it. Cousin Nathan!? He had never gotten up this early in his life!

"Shhh!" he whispered. "I'm sorry. But what I found out...you'll never believe it. I had to come and tell you. I think it's important."

"Okay," I said. "Tessa, wake up!"

Tessa and I made Nate look the other way while we put on our bathrobes. Then the three of us sat together on the sofa. It turned out Nate's mom had told him the same thing Dad told us. After that, he couldn't sleep either. So he decided to do some research online. "And," he said, "I learned something very interesting about Eb Ghanamamma's most famous folk song, 'Lina.'"

"The two of them? Really?" I said after he told us. "So that means the confederate has to be—?"

Nate nodded. "I think so."

"Let's look at the notes again," I said.

The sun still wasn't up, so we sat in the lamplight and read like we were studying for a test. It took a while, but then I spotted it, a clue we had missed all along: mud.

Piece by piece, the case came together—finally. But there was one more thing we could do to be sure. It was still dark when we tiptoed down the hall and up the stairs to the third floor.

In Nate's bedroom, the computer was the only light. He opened his e-mail and got the link Ms. Major had sent, put the volume on mute so he wouldn't wake his mom, and clicked through the Jan and Larry video till he stopped at the very last frame.

I shook my head. "I can't believe we missed that the first time."

"But what do we do now?" Tessa said. "Tell Mom? Tell Dad? What if they're going to arrest the wrong person?"

"No way," said Nate. "The grown-ups have it figured out—same as we do."

Remember how Mr. Mormora said to expect a surprise at the last Canine Class?

What he meant was Sports TV Network—STVN!

It turned out Mr. Mormora and Aunt Jen had seen a great opportunity for a story that would make the first family, the first dog and Canine Class all look good. And with Hooligan so popular, STVN loved the idea.

So that day instead of only the usual press guys watching, there were tons more cameras plus play-by-play and color commentary from two veteran sports-casters, Vin and Myron.

Having been up half the night, Tessa, Nate and I moved slowly that morning. By the time we got outside, the rest of the dogs were ready to go. With Mr. Mormora smiling and the sun shining again—it was hard to believe that after class, a diamond thief was going to be arrested.

Mr. Mormora welcomed us and also the audience watching on TV at home. Then he said, "For graduation day at Canine Class, I like to give the canines and their buddies a reward for all their work. For that reason, we are going to play a game."

The rules were easy. Each CB told his CIT to stay, then ran about fifty feet across the lawn and stopped. On the way, the CB dropped Canine Cookies. If the CIT stayed like he was supposed to, the team got a point. If he didn't—like if he tried to steal a cookie—the team lost a point. After that, the CB called, "Come!" and the CIT was supposed to run to him or her without stopping. If the CIT did it, the team got more points—one for every cookie the dog ran past.

We divided into four teams. Team One, my team, had

Ms. Major and Pickles, Mr. Bryant and Cottonball, the labradoodle and his CB, plus one of the I-don't-know-whats. Because everybody had so much confidence in Hooligan, he and I were chosen to go last.

Tessa, Nate, Granny and Dad were watching from the spectators' area as usual. Mom was in the Oval Office, as usual. Malik was over by the spectators, and Charlotte was near the STVN crew, including Myron and Vin.

"A-a-a-a-and—*go!*" said Mr. Mormora.

Mr. Bryant was first up. He told Cottonball to stay, then he started running.

Mr. Bryant is not a fast runner. But Cottonball did great. He only ate one cookie, and then it was Ms. Major's turn.

Sadly, Pickles ate every cookie! Now we were way behind—and Ms. Major was really embarrassed.

Lucky for us, the Chihuahua on Team Four was so excited he chased his tail, got dizzy and ran the wrong way. And a golden retriever on Team Three staged a sit-down strike. Finally, his CB had to carry him to the finish line.

Meanwhile, Vin and Myron narrated and kept score. When finally it was our turn, I heard: "Going into the final lap, Team One, anchored by presidential pooch Hooligan Parks, is in second place, just five points behind Team Two. Will the First Dog choke? Or will he run to victory?"

The thing about a race is—it's fun. And with the STVN excitement and the crowd, I forgot all about diamonds and bad guys and protesters. I just wanted to win!

"Go Team One!" hollered Nate from the sidelines.

"*Woo-hoo-hoo!*" hollered my drama queen sister.

I was sprinting across the South Lawn, dropping Canine Cookies as I went—and that's when I saw her: Ms. Kootoor! She had her Blueberry Bag over her shoulder, a matching sun hat on her head. She was pulling a rolling suitcase. And she was almost to the White House East Gate!

But where were the marines, the Secret Service, the D.C. police to arrest her? Didn't they know she was a diamond thief escaping?

"Hurry, Cameron! Hurry—what's the matter?" Ms. Major hollered.

I didn't know what to do. I looked over at Tessa and Nate. Couldn't they stop her? But from where they were standing, they couldn't even see her.

"What's Cameron Parks doing, Vin?" I heard Myron ask.

"Can't tell, Myron. She appears to have stopped dead in her tracks."

"Could it be a strategic move, Vin?"

"Well, she'd better move fast. The newfie-cross on Team Four is trying hard to stage a comeback!"

I dropped a cookie, ran and dropped another. Then things got worse. Ms. Kootoor was only a few yards from the East Gate, and no one seemed to care. Instead, Charlotte, Malik, a couple more Secret Service agents and three marines were all walking toward Mr. Mormora.

I got a bad feeling.

Had the grown-ups gotten it wrong? Did they think Mr. Mormora was the thief?

At the finish line, I turned back toward Hooligan, who was sitting and staying like a Top Dog to be.

"Go ahead, Cameron. Call him! Hurry up!" said Mr. Bryant.

Mr. Mormora, by now, was looking right to left as marines and officers approached. Meanwhile, Ms. Kootoor got closer and closer to the gate. The guards might stop her, but only for a moment. Everybody loved Ms. Kootoor, and she'd been going in and out for days.

If I didn't do something fast, she'd escape.

And an innocent man would be arrested!

Hooligan cocked his head. He couldn't figure out what was wrong with me either. And that's when I knew what I had to do. The whistle! It was for emergencies, wasn't it? And this was an emergency.

CHAPTER TWENTY-EIGHT

"THE girl had a powerful whistle in her pocket, don't you think so, Vin?"

"My ears are ringing, Myron. What do you suppose she's up to?"

My whistle's shriek had been followed by an echo—Tessa's. She hadn't seen Ms. Kootoor. But she knew if I had an emergency, she had an emergency, too.

Then the strangest thing happened. Every bird in every tree on the South Lawn went crazy all at once—shrieking, trilling and singing. I even heard Humdinger up in his cage: *Twee! Twee! Twee!*

A second after that, the canines started in, either howling or trying to dig down under the sound—all but Hooligan. He looked up, spotted Ms. Kootoor and forgot Canine Class altogether. So much for Top Dog—he bounded toward her at top speed. She must have known she'd never outrun him, but she dropped her suitcase and tried.

No way.

Hooligan was on her in a flash, while all the time Myron and Vin kept talking.

"What's that going on by the East Gate, Vin? Oops and ow! *That's* gotta hurt. Looks like the presidential pooch knocked down the thin lady with the big plaid purse."

"Mmm hmm, knocked the purse clean out of her hands, Myron. Did you see that?"

The shrieking whistles distracted the officers closing in on Mr. Mormora, but only for a moment. Then, when they had him surrounded, a funny thing happened. The CITs—the dogs—all looked in his direction. And next thing you know, they forgot everything they learned in Canine Class and sprang to the rescue.

Have I mentioned dogs love Mr. Mormora?

Meanwhile, I was chasing Hooligan. Even though Ms. Kootoor was a diamond thief, I couldn't let him hurt her.

Would he hurt her?

My mind was going as fast as my feet. Why had the birds gone crazy? Why had Hooligan acted different than the other dogs?

Meanwhile, a couple of Secret Service agents had peeled off to chase me, and I could hear them on their radios. "Fussbudget in jeopardy, Fussbudget in jeopardy."

Oh, *fine*. Remember how I didn't want to tell you my Secret Service code name? Tessa's is Fireball. Mine is…Fussbudget. It's what Granny calls me when I'm having a bad day.

Ms. Kootoor was on the ground when I reached her. But Hooligan didn't want to hurt her. He didn't even want to sniff her. He was all about the Blueberry Bag—trying to get his nose inside. I could see right away Ms. Kootoor wasn't dead or anything, but her stockings were torn and her jacket was dirty. I bent down, but before I could ask if she was okay, I heard Myron again.

"Vin—what do you suppose is going on there? It appears the Secret Service agents are attempting to arrest Mr. Julius Mormora."

"But the loyal canines have formed a wall of protection, Myron. They're snapping and snarling! They won't let the officers through!"

At the same time, Hooligan's head emerged from Ms. Kootoor's Blueberry Bag—and there was something familiar-looking in his mouth: a bright red diamond dog collar!

CHAPTER TWENTY-NINE

HOOLIGAN was not the Top Dog. In fact, Mr. Mormora announced that just this once, there wasn't going to be a Top Dog.

Instead, he wagged his finger at the CITs. "While all of you have made excellent progress, canines that truly have class always stay in place until their CBs release them."

I was disappointed, but Hooligan thumped his tail and smiled his doggie smile. You would have thought he got a trophy! I don't know why, but I had a funny feeling Mrs. Hedges was right. Now that Canine Class was over, he would forget all about being perfect and go back to having too much energy.

When commencement was over, Mr. Mormora waved good-bye and got into his limousine. He had a plane to catch. Oh—and it turned out his safari wasn't in the jungle at all. It was at a wild animal park in Ohio.

Myron and Vin were packing up, and the last dogs

were leaving when Tessa and Nate came over from the spectator area. Nate looked like I felt—dazed—but Tessa had a huge grin on her face. "We did it, Cammie! We solved the case, found the diamonds, and saved President Alfredo-Chin from protesters!"

I held up my hand. "High five."

"You don't seem excited," said Tessa.

"Ms Kootoor looked awfully sad when Malik put the handcuffs on her," I said.

"Did she say anything?" Tessa asked.

"*Oh*, yeah," I said. "She wanted to know how we figured it out. I told her about Nate going online and finding out about her and Mr. Ghanamamma—that they used to be sweethearts long ago, and he wrote his song 'Lina' about her. And I told her how we saw the mud on her shoes in the clip from Jan and Larry, so we knew she'd been out on the South Lawn when the diamond disappeared."

"But how did she call Hooligan from so far away?" Tessa asked.

"It was the diamond whistle," I said. "The whole thing about her dad giving it to her? She made that up. The truth is the whistle's that special kind that only dogs can hear. Dogs and birds, that is. While she was staying in the White House, she trained Hooligan to come whenever he heard it. For a reward, she used cut-up hot dogs!'

"So that's what was in the cooler," Nate said.

"Oh!" said Tessa. "And when Hooligan went crazy?

And knocked over Mrs. Hedges? Ms. Kootoor must have blown the whistle. We couldn't hear it, but Humdinger and Hooligan did."

"That's what I figured, too," I said. "Then today when I blew the whistle, Hooligan ran for Ms. Kootoor— just the way she'd trained him. He must've expected there'd be hot dogs in the Blueberry Bag. But instead, he found this." The collar had been in my pocket for safe-keeping. Now I pulled it out. With all twelve diamonds, it sparkled in the sunlight. Pretty soon either Charlotte or Malik or the guys in gray suits would take it. But for now? I bent down and buckled it on Hooligan's neck.

He raised his nose in the air. He knew he looked handsome.

"Ms. Kootoor told me one more thing," I said. "She didn't do it for the money. She did it for love."

"*Awwww,*" said Tessa.

"*Ewwww,*" said Nate.

"But there are still some things I don't understand," said Tessa. "Like—"

Surrounded by aides and Secret Service agents, here came Mom striding toward us through the Rose Garden. "*Mama-a-a-a!*" Tessa called, and the two of us ran to meet her.

"Good news, girls. The security alert has been lifted," Mom said. "So things will be getting back to normal around here."

"What's normal?" I asked.

"Madam President?" said one of her aides. "Excuse

me, Madam President?" said another. "It's very important that we—" "You have a meeting in five minutes, do
you realize—" "There's an urgent call from—"

Mom squinched her eyes shut, took a deep breath
and held up her hand. Instantly, her aides stopped talking. "Muffins?" she said. "If the weather holds, I am
planning a family picnic for noon today on the Oval
Office patio. How does that sound?"

Her aides started to protest. Three mayors and an
admiral were waiting! And what about the walnut blight
in Michigan? Mom raised her hand again. "After lunch,"
she said.

"Is Granny invited?" Tessa asked.

"Of course," Mom said.

"Then you'd better invite Mr. Bryant," Tessa said.

"Mr. Bryant?" Mom said.

"We'll catch you up," I said.

It stayed sunny, so we got to eat on the patio—
sandwiches, cole slaw, drinks, fruit salad and cookies.

Dad raised a glass of cider. "To Cammie and Tessa
and Nate!" he said. "Without their hard work and detecting, the wrong person would now be in jail."

We all raised our glasses, but—like me—Mom
didn't look that happy. "Are you sad because Ms. Kootoor was your friend?" I asked her.

"You get knocked around a lot when you're in politics," Mom said, "even by your friends. I'm getting
pretty tough, but yes, it makes me sad."

"Do you think Ms. Kootoor and Eb Ghanamamma really wanted to help the people?" I asked.

"Possibly," Mom said. "But they sure went about it the wrong way."

"A few more things are bugging me," I said. "Like was the 'heightened security' because of the missing diamonds?"

"And is that what you were spending all your time on, Mama?" Tessa asked.

"I can't tell you everything yet," said Mom. "But generally? Yes and yes. Just like you girls and Granny, my security team realized pretty quickly that there was a connection between El Brillante and the diamonds on Hooligan's collar. So they started looking into it. All the evidence seemed to point to Mr. Mormora, and we knew he was leaving today. With time running out, they decided to arrest him, but they had to keep it quiet. And of course we wanted to wait till after Canine Class."

"What everybody missed was the old romance between Ms. Kootoor and Eb Ghanamamma," Dad explained. "And I, for one, can't believe I didn't put that together. When he sang 'Lina,' there were rumors it was about a famous American model. But I never thought how Lina could be a nickname for Madeline."

"There's more things I don't get," Tessa said. "Like how come only one diamond was missing, and then the whole collar?"

"My guess," Mom said, "is that the thief had to prove to her buyer that the diamonds were what she said they were. She took one, hoping it wouldn't be missed."

"And what about the Canine Cookies Hooligan found?" I asked.

Granny answered that one. "I think Ms. Kootoor took that box from the outdoor shed, then dropped cookies here and there. She was in the kitchen and heard you talking Saturday morning, remember? She must have thought if she dropped the cookies, you'd suspect Mr. Mormora instead of her."

"Ahem?" One of Mom's aides had come across the lawn. He was holding a phone. You could tell he was embarrassed to interrupt.

Mom reached for the phone. "What is it?"

"Oh—it's not for you, ma'am. It's for the children." He held the phone out. "It's on speaker."

A voice said, "Hello? Am I speaking to the children of the president of the United States?"

"Hey, President Alfredo-Chin!" said Tessa. "How ya doin'?"

"Very well, thank you," answered the voice. "Although we have had a difficult time here in our nation. Now, I am confident things will be better. So I call to thank you for your efforts."

"You're welcome!" said Tessa, Nate and I.

"And when the time is right," President Alfredo-Chin went on, "I am planning to bring my dog, Empress Pu-Chi, to your country for a visit. I know how very much she would enjoy meeting your handsome dog, Hooligan."

Nate, Tessa and I looked at each other. After what

Mr. Mormora had said, we didn't expect we'd like the empress very much. But then we shrugged and said in a chorus "*Sure!*" It didn't really matter, did it? What were the chances the president of a nearby nation would ever bring his dog to Washington, D.C.?

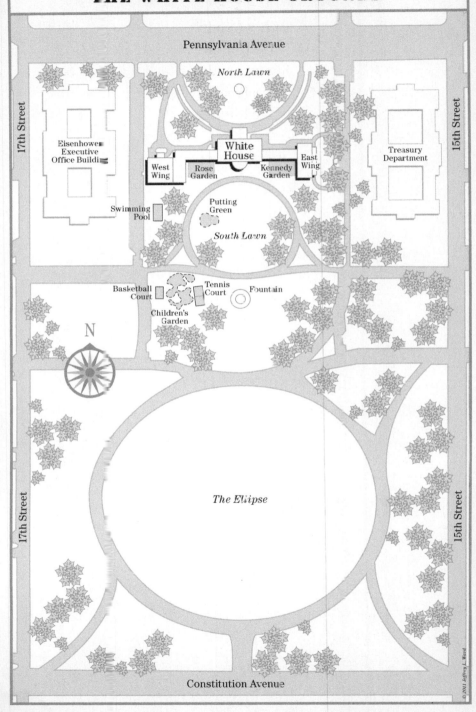

AFTERWORD

THE South Lawn of the White House is the backyard for the president's family.

And what a great backyard!

Together with the smaller North Lawn in front, it takes up eighteen acres—the size of a dozen football fields.

The South Lawn includes plenty of beautiful trees, some of them dedicated by presidents long ago. The oldest still standing are two southern magnolias next to the South Portico (the White House backdoor), planted in 1830 by President Andrew Jackson in memory of his wife, Rachel. They usually flower in June.

And speaking of flowers, thousands bloom on the grounds every year. In the spring, more than forty thousand grape hyacinths and oxford tulips bloom around the two fountains alone. John Quincy Adams, president from 1825 to 1829, planted the first gardens and wrote in his diary about two acres covered with at least a thousand "forest and fruit-trees, shrubs, hedges, esculent (edible) vegetables, kitchen and medicinal herbs, hot-house plants, flowers, and weeds."

Today, a twenty-person National Park Service crew takes care of the White House grounds, and it's a lot of work. Just mowing the lawn takes eight hours in warm weather, and has to be done twice a week. In charge of it all is the superintendent, who has an office on the ground floor of the White House. Most days he gets to work at six a.m.

And while fictional White House pooch Hooligan has Mr. Bryant to watch over him, real White House pets are often looked after by the White House gardeners and groundskeepers.

Of course, the South Lawn isn't just for pets and plants. Like any backyard, it's also for fun!

In the 1920s President Herbert Hoover often invited his advisers to have breakfast and play a game of "Hoover Ball" on the lawn for exercise. Many presidents have enjoyed golf, and near the president's office in the West Wing is a putting green. The first one was installed in 1954, and the squirrels liked it as much as President Dwight Eisenhower did. He blamed the critters on the president before him, Harry Truman, who enjoyed feeding them by hand.

Along with the putting green, there is a swimming pool, tennis courts and horseshoe pitch—all put in by different presidents to suit their favorite pastimes. In 2009, for example, President Barack Obama had the lines on one tennis court repainted so it could also be used for full-court basketball.

Of course it's not just grown-ups who get to play in the big backyard. President Franklin D. Roosevelt's grandchildren, Sistie and Buzz, had a slide, jungle gym and swing on the east side of the lawn. The Kennedy children had playground sets, as do Sasha and Malia Obama. President Jimmy Carter's daughter, Amy, had her own treehouse.

Also for children is a special garden installed in 1968 by President Lyndon Johnson and his wife. Tucked away near the tennis courts, it features a gold-fish pond, child-size outdoor furniture and an apple tree for climbing. Bronze castings of the footprints and handprints of presidents' children and grandchildren are embedded in the paving stones of the garden's path.

The Children's Garden is one of three on the South Lawn. The other two—the Rose Garden and the Jacqueline Kennedy Garden, which is sometimes called the First Ladies Garden—are larger. Where today's Rose Garden is located, stables and greenhouses once stood. You can see this garden on TV quite a lot because it's used for news conferences and other events like the president's annual pardoning of the turkey at Thanks-giving. Visitors on White House tours get to see Mrs. Kennedy's garden through the windows as they walk along the East Wing colonnade.

The White House is often called "the people's house," and presidents say it belongs to all Americans. Still, the president would have a hard time getting any work done if all Americans felt free to drop by anytime. When President Jackson was sworn into office in 1829, he had an open house to celebrate—and twenty thousand guests showed up! They made such a mess that no one knew what to do, until the president ordered orange punch to be served from washtubs on the lawn. When the guests went out to get a drink, the staff closed the doors on them.

To visit the president's backyard today, you have to make special arrangements or else have an invitation. One tradition that brings a lot of visitors is the annual Easter Egg Roll on the Monday after the holiday. Another tradition was started by President George W. Bush, who once owned a baseball team. Every year, he invited Little League T-ball players for a game on the lawn. When First Lady Michelle Obama oversaw the planting of a kitchen garden in 2009, she invited Washington, D.C., schoolchildren to help her.

If you'd like to see the White House grounds for yourself, visit www.WhiteHouse.gov. There you will find information about garden tours, entering the lottery for tickets to the Easter Egg Roll. Even if you're not lucky enough to get an invitation to the president's backyard, you can get a view from E Street in Washington, D.C.